EARTHSHINE

NEIL THOMPSON

Published by New Generation Publishing in 2012

First Edition

Cover design by Ryan Thompson

Gaetano Donizetti (1797 – 1848) – 'Bella Siccome un Angelo', *Don Pasquale*

Georges Bizet (1838 – 1875) – 'Votre Toast Je Peux Vous le Rendre' (The Toreador's Song), *Carmen*

www.newgeneration-publishing.com

 **New Generation Publishing**

For Janet, Ryan and especially Robyn

And for precious Rhys who began this novel, and journey,
with me,
'Unto the pure all things are pure'

About The Author

Neil Thompson was brought up in the former South West Africa (present day Namibia) and has lived there for many years. He is a very experienced traveller and has spent time with many people from a wide range of backgrounds and origins. This has directly influenced his writing in capturing cultures and locations. His debut novel, *Running Before that Wind* was published in 2010 by Matador.

Acknowledgements:

I would like to thank David Grubb for his continued encouragement; Mair Huggard for the correct phrases and words in Welsh and for her help. The maps and drawings were done by Andrew Morrison – my gratitude goes to him, and also for his always cheerful support.

CONTENTS

MAP OF MALI

GLOSSARY (in order of appearance)

Marabout	Muslim holy man
Tuareg	Traditionally nomadic people who roamed the Sahara
Koevoet	Controversial and predominantly black South West African Police
Dakar	Capital City of Senegal
Tamacheq	Language of the Tuareg
Mouflon	Wild mountain goat (North Africa)
Toubab	White man/white person
Bella	A group who originated as slaves or servants of the dominant Tuareg
Fulani	The Fula, also called Fulani, one of the most widespread of West African people
Dogon	Intriguing group of people, found along the Bandiagara Escarpment in Mali
Bambara	The largest ethnic group in Mali
Songhaï	A group of people living predominantly in Niger and northern Mali
Caprivi	Area of land, north-eastern Namibia (prev. South West Africa)
Ovambo	A large ethnic group in Namibia
Myrrh	A fragrant gum resin (sweet cicely)
Ihaggaren	Tuareg noble class
Harmattan	Very dry, dusty wind
Toubou	Ethnic group that live mainly in Northern Chad
Tibesti	Mountainous area (Northern Chad)

Pied d'elephant Tree	False abura tree (common name)
Burkinabé	The people of Burkina Faso
Olibanum	Frankincense
Keffiyeh	A headdress worn by Arab men
Bashir	Omar al-Bashir - president of Sudan
Neem	Also known as Dogon Yaro, a tree in the mahogany family
Bush Taxi	Mini bus (often in very poor condition)
Tombouctou	Also Timbuktu, frontier town in Mali
Shebeen	Unlicensed establishment selling alcoholic drink (especially South Africa)
Ti-in Essako	Village, Eastern Mali (border area Mali/Niger/Algeria)
Madrassa	A college for Islamic instruction
Wheatear	Desert Wheatear , small sandy-coloured bird
Samovar	Highly decorated tea urn
Armoire	Ornate or antique cupboard or wardrobe
Takhi	Mongolian wild horse, also known as Przewalski's horse

Tuareg Proverbs

'Houses are the graves of the living'

'Where water flows freely,
people live in affluence'

'God has opened our mouths to put into them two things,
either food to live or sand to die'

PART 1

DAVID AND TECWWA

Chapter 1
Rescue

He was seldom lucid now.

It had been slow in coming, but he knew now that his body was shutting down. His life spirit was flickering. In another day or two he would die, probably unconscious then dead. Or they would just kill him.

The guard designated to look after him, Ahmed, had to support him when he urinated or defecated. Even then his waste was so little, urine a dark blood-coloured yellow, faeces like dried rabbit pellets.

He had been held captive for so long. Time, days, months, had become meaningless. There was nothing to be desired: no hunger, no thirst. His quest for freedom had virtually faded away, was now almost dormant.

A white man incarcerated in the harshest of environments, deep in the Sahara. His capture by Islamic bandits.

All this had doomed him.

He knew it.

Everything was startlingly clear in the brief moments when he was alert. Remembrance of long forgotten incidents from his youth, dates of meetings and events going back years, surnames of people whom he may have met only once, old sporting results.

He listened as the negotiator, the Marabout, spoke to his captors for the last time.

'There is no money, no agreement. His government refuses to pay.'

'The infidel will be slaughtered.'

The Arabic words were difficult to follow, but he knew

enough to understand.

Through the blindfold he could sense Ahmed's eyes turned towards him. Was there compassion, a feeling of sympathy, or merely an acknowledgement that his fate had been determined?

It was late and very quiet, the men asleep in their blankets around the ebbing fire. The intense desert cold had brought him out of delirium. Or was it something else? A sound, like a muted gurgle, a faint noise out of place. There was a light touch on his shoulder, a whisper where the blindfold crossed his ear.

'*Brawd bach*, keep very quiet, keep the faith; *ons het jou kom haal.*'

'Come to fetch me?' Was he dreaming, hallucinating, wishing words into his head? Imagining release yet again.

Yet there was only one man that would mix Welsh, English and South African Afrikaans in a single sentence and in the knowledge that he would understand.

Whitey le Roux; here?

He felt himself being lifted, drawn up across a wide set of shoulders. There was a steadying moment as the man carrying him got the weight right. A broad balancing stride and they were off into the desert.

After what seemed to be an hour, but in fact took much longer, the big man lowered him gently to the ground.

A trickle of water passed over his lips, the blindfold was removed. A knife cut the ropes binding his hands and legs.

'We would have done this earlier, but it was easier to carry you still tied up.'

He looked around. It was getting lighter as dawn began to break.

Whitey was kneeling with a water bottle. Three other men stood around, two of them dressed in the long flowing royal-blue robes and wrap-around face veils that only the Tuareg men wear; the third, the man who had carried him, a black giant with a large white toothed smile.

And then they all moved aside.

She looked, and then was down beside him. Her soft clear voice shook as she spoke.

'My dear one, you are still alive. We will never be separated again. My world is behind me.'

Chapter 2
Mali

The panorama from the window revealed a view of an open pit that had grown even wider and deeper during these last years. Spiralling down, the access roads seemed to diminish ever narrower. At the bottom of the mine the great haul trucks and excavators looked like toys in motion.

'Four years,' he thought, 'time gone in a flash.'

'David, are you ok?' Roger MacArthur, the man who was replacing him, asked.

'Yes, fine, Roger, just a last look and then I'm out of here.'

'I'll leave you on your own for a few minutes. Just want to check today's test results in the lab.'

'Thank you.'

Standing there a little longer, David wondered what lay ahead of him.

One thing he was sure of, this was the end of working for a large international conglomerate. He yearned for a simpler life. One not driven by bean counters in suits and ties, not driven by returns on investment and adding value to shareholders funds. And not driven by corporate greed to make business less humane.

The maximising of profit was affecting his employees' lives. Even though he had been so successful, David knew that he was now at the point of finding difficulty in conforming. He knew that his own ethics were being compromised, had felt it these few last years.

Maybe this was the so-called mid-life crisis; or maybe it was just time to say no and move on.

David sat there looking down, watching the ore being carted to the surface. But of course, there was more to it than that. Deep within himself he knew that he had to change. He was starting to become more introspective, even slightly reclusive, finding that memories of his childhood were starting to affect him.

At church on Sunday mornings our stepfather would stand with his hands on our shoulders. A paternal contact that drew appreciative glances from the immediate surrounding congregation. My sister, forever emotionally disturbed because of him, would inwardly tremble, quake under his touch.

By twelve o'clock that same day, he and my mother would be in the local bar, returning two hours later when it closed. Joined by one or two other couples, the loud music and raucous carousing would commence. Or sometimes they would gamble, playing various forms of poker.

Quietly my sister would prepare sandwiches and tea; for the two of us to eat in the garage. Our Sunday lunch together away from them.

In the early evenings we would creep into our bedrooms. Once I went to get a glass of water. After that, never again. In his undershorts, drunk and spread-eagled on the couch was my stepfather, a woman, not my mother, next to him, her naked breasts flattened by the sprawl of his arm. And passing a bedroom on my return, I could hear Mother's encouraging whimpers followed by guttural grunting sounds.

Over the years, the few lady friends who had also been David's lovers were all intelligent and caring women. They could never understand that deep conviction within him: a belief that formal marriage, baptism, confirmation, churchgoing was superficial, most times hypocritical. A religious covering-up of many things wrong.

Out there, somewhere, would something be different. He was sure of it. Another way of living which would help settle his mind, reinstate personal values within him that he felt were becoming increasingly eroded. Perhaps, one day, a woman to share a future life with.

He had fantasised about what he wanted to do. To others it would seem so daunting, to explore remote areas, travel where few white people go. There was plenty to see, old towns and cities, fabled places where ancient kingdoms had grown and flourished. Far-flung, almost unreachable, unknown to many.

But now seeing what he had been part of, he felt saddened. So much that he had helped to plan and develop and manage. Now he was leaving.

Pensively his mind flashed back in memory, episodes and occurrences mainly from his first year in control.

'David, I need you to go to Mali. Get our new operation into shape,' his managing director Mike Shannon stated.

'But what about Lee and his assistant? They're both good men.'

'I'm bringing them back as soon as you get there.'

'Assuming I'll go, of course.'

Mike's rough-hewn near-sighted face peered at David belligerently.

'Of course, you're bloody going. I'll agree to almost anything; four year contract, performance bonus, profit share, you just name it.'

'Full board membership for the four years?'

'Why the fuck do you want that?'

'So that I get to hear what you think of me. First hand every three months. And that if you ignore me from a distance I get a chance to rectify it in front of the chairman.'

'Why would I ignore you? You're my top man. The best man manager in this whole frigging business.'

Mike smiled, turning on the charm.

'Please David; I need tonnages up. And costs down. And a more settled workforce. The Malians are giving us too much political pressure. The workers are unhappy, the natives are fucking restless. It's a volcano about to blow.'

He knew that he had made a sale.

During the first months Mike phoned David nearly every day from wherever he found himself, whether in his Johannesburg office or on holiday.

His grizzled technical director, a former mining engineer would visit every few weeks.

After each visit there would be the inevitable eruptive telephone call.

'What's this about changing shifts?' Mike screeched.

'Yes, we're changing from two ten hour shifts to continuous shifts, three by eight hours.'

'From when? We must discuss it first. Work the numbers.'

'From last Monday. I've done the numbers. Read my last report again.'

'But what about the operators and drivers? They won't agree to earning less money.'

'They will,' David said.

There was a frozen stillness. 'What?'

'If we meet production targets they'll get a bonus, bringing their earnings up to an equivalent of a ten hour shift. At least the same as they were earning before, more if production is higher. And, if my planning works out we can employ more people which will please the local governor.'

'Jesus, I'll have to get Human Resources out there fast.'

'Too late, and not necessary,' David replied, 'all signed and sealed. Oh, and another thing.'

This time there was no icy query. Just silence.

'You need to remove haul truck 7. Take it off site, off the books; head office can carry the depreciation costs.'

'Why?'

'We don't need it. It's mothballed. Send it back to the suppliers, cancel the agreements.'

'Bloody Hell, David, how the heck am I going to do that? It's a huge amount of capital to re-organise.'

'The suppliers helped with the plant configuration for this site. Tell them to sort it out. They got it wrong.'

One of the big first day surprises then had been the Chief of Security.

'Fokken hell, David, out of which aardvark hole did you crawl?'

'Whitey le Roux!' David exclaimed. 'It must have been all of twenty five years ago.'

'Ja, in those days I was the boss and you were the *troepie*. Now you're the boss and I'm the bloody *troepie*.'

And he laughed and stuck his hand out. Shaking it was like holding a piece of rough granite attached to a wrought iron corded bar.

'Remember those days, boss. Angola and Koevoet, bombs and mortars dropping out of nowhere. This place is like a nursery school picnic.'

He looked and was the same as all those years ago. Hard, tough, fearless and loyal.

'Whitey, I hear the workforce is unsettled, want to strike, have threatened to sabotage the fleet.'

'It's the previous managers, boss. They don't know how to listen to a person. They talked, pretended to listen and didn't hear. Feedback means fuck all to them. But I remember you. You've more brains than all of us. You'll sort it out in no time.'

Whitey's eyes gave lead to his nickname. They were so pale, a precise shade of incandescent grey under his thick blond hair. When he took his sunglasses off it was like looking at a welding arc. Those eyes pierced: his enemies, and those scared of him, turned away at his glare.

Whitey and his wife Marie became the closest friends David

could have had. The bonds forged all those years ago in their Army Service, strengthened day by day.

And so the changes went on. The haul roads were widened and dust suppression enhanced. Berms were built higher; production increased and stockpiles grew. Equipment maintenance costs dropped lower. Accidents reduced to almost zero.

David attended the company's board meetings in South Africa. Steadily the financial results improved as well.

His own life settled too. David had never married. He and his last girlfriend had called it a day some time ago, their separation as he moved from contract to contract, country to country, pulling them apart. She wanted to settle in one place and have a family. Even before his placement in Mali these last four years they had known it was over. He was still not ready for marriage.

Life on a mine tended to settle into a steady routine. Everything became almost militarily organised. With an expatriate community at the core of the workforce, things were always done in the same established and predictable way.

There were tennis afternoons, squash leagues and chess evenings. There were football matches featuring admin, plant, operator and drivers teams. There were monthly dances, annual year end parties. And there were awards for everything, operator of the month, driver of the month, employee of the year and so on.

The Mine Manager was God. Paternalistic, autocratic, disciplinarian, usually difficult, high profile, always deferred to.

David took the other route. Reserved, quiet and relaxed. Played social tennis and squash, enjoying it even though he was easily the best player. Ran most evenings along the dusty trucks towards the nearest settlements, sometimes accompanied by the local village boys or a few of the operators. They all knew who he was, but it made no difference.

The women were left alone. There was always one with an itch to scratch or a point to prove.

And the telephone call at the end of the fourth month.

'What the hell is your Chief Storeman doing in my office? Six thousand bloody miles away from where he should be!' Mike Shannon shouted.

'I've sent him back.'

'I know that. But why?'

'His stores are a shambles. There is far too much stock. Of everything. And I'm convinced he's on the take from suppliers. That's why the inventory is so high. There is stuff here that we won't use in ten years.'

'What about his wife?'

'She left last month. She can't stand him anymore either.'

'David, David, this is the chairman's nephew we are talking about,' Mike's voice lowered.

'I know. He told me that too.'

'Where am I going to find you another man at such short notice?'

'You won't have to. I've already employed somebody locally. She started three days ago.'

'A woman storeman! On a mine. Are you crazy or is there something going on?' The innuendo implied.

'Yes, there is,' David replied coolly. 'She's the local chief's sister, married to our best machine driver, speaks very good English and takes no nonsense from anyone. Miriam's in her mid fifties, children all grown up, with a good sense of how this operation works. I think she's just about right.'

'Oh David, you always have the bloody answer.'

There were the difficult and sad times as well.

European men who couldn't keep their hands off the local Mali women. The German mechanics in particular. They seemed to have an uncontrolled lust for women of colour. When a plump Bavarian was killed by an irate and jealous suitor, the difficult part was explaining it all to the dead man's wife.

And operators who contracted AIDS, shunned by their family communities and fellow workers. The personnel officer committing suicide when his wife left him for the smooth sweet-talking French doctor.

Examining the reflection in that panoramic window, David could see that he had aged as well. Hair going a little grey, lines on his face that had not been there when he had first arrived.

Turning, shaking hands with those in the offices, he was out the gate and into a new life.

Everyone said that he had left a legacy; to David it was the last and most rewarding job. He had done what he had set out to do.

Chapter 3
Moussa

There were basically five types of people who emerge from the slums of Dakar.

There was the inhabitant who lived day by day, maybe working as a part-time gardener or helper at some backyard mechanic. There was the woman that bartered to keep her family alive, fruit for fish, a cap for a baby's dress.

Sometimes she would sleep with the baker in exchange for a little flour. There was the hawker along the street, flogging whatever he could get his hands on; cheap Chinese sunglasses and watches, telephone cards, cashew nuts and wedges of processed cheese. There were the con men and connivers, wheeling and dealing in scams and illegal services.

And then there was Moussa. Along with Whitey le Roux, the most honest, steadfast and trustworthy man David had ever met. A middle child in amongst ten, Moussa found a school he could go to; with inner intelligence he knew that he had to better himself in order to help his family.

He once took David to the reeking slum where his mother stayed, his father having died some years before.

David was humbled, chastened by what he saw that humid, stifling day.

Their tiny home was crowded by makeshift shacks on three sides and fronted by a dusty, pitted and filth strewn road.

Seven people lived in those two meagre rooms. A third room, only partly completed and open on two sides, formed a sitting area. There was a bed in one corner, with a hessian screen around it.

'That is where my Mama sleeps,' Moussa explained, 'the rest of our family... the boys have one room, the girls the other.'

'And you?' David asked.

'I sleep in my taxi.'

'Every night?'

'Yes, every night.'

The place was so small. No running water, no electricity and no toilet. Cooking was done outside over an open fire.

The surrounding external conditions were disgusting, undrained and dirty, where litter, both paper and putrid waste lay everywhere. Yet when inspected closely, that little part-built shack was spotless. A few ornaments positioned neatly on a ledge, photographs of family members hanging level and square on nails in the walls. Everything clean, with its own place.

And it was not just like that for David's benefit; it was always like that. When one met Moussa's mother, one saw a proud, polite and gracious matriarch whose qualities had passed on to her son.

Moussa learnt to drive and became a taxi driver. He persuaded the taxi owner to let him patrol the hotels. There another thing was learned: he had to improve his linguistic skills. Phrase books were borrowed, languages practised with his passengers: the diplomats, businessmen and tourists who visited Senegal.

English, French, reasonable German, a smattering of Spanish and Italian. Wolof, Fula, Jolla and surprisingly fair Tamacheq, language of the desert dwelling, nomadic Tuareg.

'How did you learn Tamacheq?' David asked just after meeting him.

'There is one, a Tuareg who lives near me. He makes silver jewellery. Sells to the tourists. Everyday I pick him up, bring him to the city centre. He taught me.'

David offered Moussa a job, with conditions that he would later not be able to fully honour.

His plans were to spend three years touring North and West Africa. Visiting the remote and fascinating areas.

The offer was simple.

'Travel with me. Be my driver, guide and translator. I'll double your present wage, pay all your costs, three weeks annual leave. And at the end I'll give you my Land Rover plus a cash bonus.'

In the light of what he currently earned, which was about thirty US dollars a month, Moussa's acceptance would make him, by local standards, a wealthy man.

Tall and upright like many Senegalese, he looked at David, his large brown eyes wide in surprise and wonder.

'I am thirty five years now, Boss. In a minute you have changed my life. And that of my family. I can now afford to take a wife and maybe, one day, build my own house.'

He shook David's hand, the contract sealed.

Their expeditions took them across Senegal, into the Casamance and up to the Koba. They met people that could speak no other language than their own: wild animals isolated into areas under minimal protection.

Hiking up in the Bassari country and in the Fouta Doulon brought unspoilt landscapes and vistas.

Fishing for barracuda in the Bijagos Archipelago was beyond Moussa. He had never learnt to swim and was scared of the sea. He waited in Bubaque while David spent a month fishing and looking for pygmy hippos, sea turtles and seldom seen manatees.

They travelled through Togo, Benin and Ghana, then back into Mali where David had last worked. David paid courtesy visits to the mine and spent a few days every so often with Whitey and Marie le Roux.

Chapter 4
Contraband

It was the desert travel that David really enjoyed. Long days of nothing and then came a sudden surprise. A cave with rock art painted thousands of years ago, small hidden oases, a fleeting glimpse of an oryx or mouflon.

All the arid lands were so very different to him. The dry and extremely barren Atacama down South America's Pacific coastline; running for thousands of kilometres; nothing of interest, nothing to see.

The fascinating Gobi with vast areas covered in stone pebbles and chips; the stone pavements through which the nomadic Mongols moved with their large herds of horses and sheep.

The Pinacate Sonora, surrounded by a volcanic landscape of many different sized calderas. From the top of Pinacate David had looked down – a vista of mainland Mexico, Sea of Cortez, Baja Peninsula and to the far right, the Pacific Ocean, all in one spectacular outlook.

There was plenty of life in the Kalahari. In the sand river beds, animals sheltered from the sun under large camelthorn trees: lions, cheetah, eland and hartebeest. Sometimes in the selfsame trees were leopards or a giant eagle owl. Hyena lay in the waterholes with their prey submerged for preservation.

When rain fell in the Namib the grass grew, by appearance, overnight. A brilliant emerald green carpet in which springbok and zebra thrived.

The Sahara: the world's great desert. Extensive sand seas, thousands of yellow-orange dunes, mountainous rock formations and many diverse tribes: some wandering and itinerant, others now settled in a more pastoral way of life. They still yearned for their old ways but reluctantly realised those days were long gone.

One thing was certain. Living in these lands was difficult. A desert dweller's psyche knew that drought had no meaning. There could be wind, vicious swirling sandstorms that scour the landscape. There were extremes of temperature, searingly high, bitingly cold. There were mirages that confused sight and mind. The rain-moments were far between: sometimes flash flooding, sometimes nothing at all for years.

From the top of the eastern Bandiagara Falaise David looked down. He could see Moussa below, sitting in the shade of the Land Rover. In the far distance, to the left, were some palm trees indicating the village settlement where they planned to camp that night.

He walked along the plateau for about three hundred metres and angled his way down a ravine. Maybe he would find a hidden pool for a wash before rejoining his driver and now good friend.

The sound seemed to come from all sides as he descended.

'Ugh...ugh...ugh...uugh'

It was a hurt hoarse sound amplified without character or distinction. About half way down David intersected a narrow sand and rock-packed path. Following it and steadily making his way lower, he came across them.

A man lay on the path wedged under a huge boulder. He had a rope wrapped around his arm. The weight at the end of the rope was dragging him ever more tightly, his torso slowly and inevitably being crushed. Around the corner, off the track, lay a camel too, still fully laden.

A quick assessment made David wonder why the nomad had chosen such a difficult and unsuitable route. He must have been leading the animal when it slipped. Now lying on the slope, another large rock had stopped the camel falling any further. In a frenzy, the poor creature tugged on the lead rope.

With a few slashes of his knife David hacked the rope in two and helped the hurt man to one side. He collapsed there groaning, unable to move. David had a sense that there were some cracked ribs. The man's right leg was bent at an unnatural angle and looked to be badly broken above the knee.

Secured by where it lay and weighted down by the load being carried, the camel sprawled immobile, legs hanging freely on either side of the rock.

David left the injured duo, making his way to an open space. 'Bring rope,' he shouted down to Moussa. 'Plus the first aid kit!'

Moussa looked up and David waved.

'Bring rope and the first aid kit. And tent poles!' He shouted again.

There was no question or hesitation. Twenty minutes later Moussa was with him.

He spoke to the injured man and between them they forced half a dozen painkillers down his throat.

'We must get the baggage off the camel,' Moussa said. 'The man says we mustn't lose the goods otherwise we all will die.'

'What does that mean?' David questioned.

His Senegalese companion shook his shoulders.

But it soon became evident as to why. The camel was carrying about one hundred and twenty kilograms in weight; one hundred and twenty kilograms of AK47s, machine pistols and ammunition. And as they loosened the baggage, another layer became evident; fifty bags of neatly-packed white powder, each weighing about half a kilogram.

Scrambling off the path, they scouted around looking for a small cave. Finding one, the contraband was stacked and concealed under a mound of rocks, which in turn was covered with some cut branches from a nearby scrubby tree.

By now the stricken animal could feel that the burden was gone. Watching the men with fear-filled eyes, the camel's front legs tried to find some footing. However it couldn't even roll a little in an attempt to get onto its knees.

Moussa and David tied a rope around its upper body and underneath the legs, attempting to haul it to its feet. This didn't work. They tried to drag the rear of the animal's body up the track in an endeavour to free its back legs. This proved to be equally futile. The camel was inextricably jammed, and rigid with fear.

By now both men had severe rope burns on their arms. David's shirt was torn away and he also had a deep lash-cut on his back. Blood flowed freely down into his trousers.

There were muttered words from the man on the ground. From beneath his robes he drew out a 38mm revolver.

'David, you must shoot it,' Moussa said.

He knew what had to be done. Not an easy thing to do. Taking his time and drawing a deep breath, he bent down next to the camel. He held the pistol close to its temple, turned away and pulled the trigger.

The sound reverberated around the ravine. The animal's head reared up, there were several anguished feeble grunts as it convulsed into death. David could not look at it.

Moussa put his hand on his shoulder. A sincere sympathy.

For a few moments they stood there gathering themselves, before turning back to the hurt nomad. With the tent poles and rope they formed a makeshift stretcher. Stumbling downward and almost totally exerted, Moussa and David carried him to the Land Rover. The man's agony loud and evident whenever they stumbled.

From there they drove to the settlement which David had seen from the top of the escarpment.

At first appearance the village seemed to be inhabited mainly by Bella and a few Tuaregs. The men in their distinctive black and blue robes and turbans gathered around when they arrived. They took the hurt man from the two strangers and laid him on the ground. There seemed to be an urgent animated fear about the group.

'They are asking him about the guns,' Moussa whispered to David. 'He is one of them. It must be part of a trade.'

'Tell them what happened,' David said.

Moussa stepped forward. They all stood back, stopped to listen to what he had to say.

There was a rush of activity when he finished speaking. Within minutes some of the men left, driving donkeys ahead of them back up the escarpment track.

Only then did two women, both shrouded in black, come forward. Looking at the injured man, they instructed the remaining onlookers to carry him to a mud hut some distance from the village itself.

One of the women circled the two newcomers. David sensed she was examining their lacerations and bruises. There was a sympathetic intake of breath; she must have seen his back.

She spoke a few words and the men were led away to a vacant building where two sleeping mats were placed on the floor. Now stiff and sore, David tried to make himself comfortable. Moussa was equally tired, but he fussed over his friend, making sure he was cared for to some degree.

Then sleep took over.

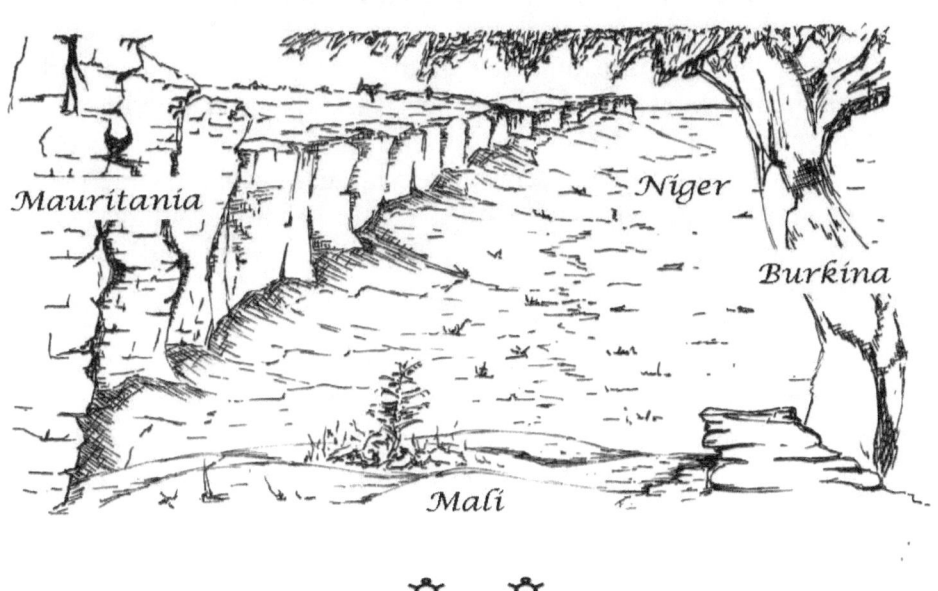

Chapter 5
Tecwwa

She usually treated only women. They came to her for a variety of complaints, ranging from pre-menstrual cramps to headaches, fevers and unknown lumps. Sometimes she acted as midwife, other times a marriage consultant, always in confidence and always to be trusted.

Very occasionally men would be referred to her. Usually for a broken arm or damaged hand, suffered when a fractious camel or donkey reared out of control.

Now, in the space of a few hours Tecwwa was faced with three men to treat, the last of which was a white man without a shirt on.

She had last touched a semi-nude man, her husband, more than twenty years ago when they still lived in her home village, just before he was killed at the beginning of the second Tuareg rebellion.

A white man had never been under her hands.

His back was lightly tanned. She could see the difference in his arms which were umber-brown. The muscles were also sharply defined. Solid shoulders tapering smoothly over blades and into the posterior, strong muscularity along each side of his spine. His waist was tight; and although big and strong, there was no excess to him. This came as a surprise as she recalled the overweight European tourists she had occasionally observed travelling through the desert areas.

Rope weals were clear where he had wrestled and struggled with the poor doomed camel. The worst lay in the centre; a

36

diagonal cut stretching twenty-five centimetres long, nearly three centimetres deep through the dermis and muscle.

From experience she knew that the wound should be stitched together, something that could only be done at the nearest clinic. But the clinic was many hours drive away and the problem needed dealing with now, before infection set in and whilst the skin and flesh was still pliable.

She turned to her friend Tana, her only friend and trainee helper, and whispered a few words.

Moussa was firmly told to stay outside.

The medicine woman was ready to begin.

David could feel the pain. It was burning, intensely sharp. He flinched and groaned quietly when she first touched him.

What seemed like a thick piece of leather was placed carefully between his teeth. It seemed to have been coated in something opiate, narcotic – a barbiturate that he could taste. He slowly felt himself slipping away, almost asleep again.

As he drifted off, a paste was spread over and through the cut. It seemed to deaden the area, but then unconsciousness took over and David felt nothing more.

With a clean soft cotton cloth she wiped the excess paste off. The water that her helper had boiled on the fire outside was cooler now.

She washed the area carefully, swabbed all the blood away until the cut was open and clean. With a piece of smooth wood, a homemade spatula, she coated the damage with a viscous solution that Tana had prepared.

Tecwwa started stitching. The needle was large, normally used for tent making, one that she had inherited from her mother so many years ago. The thread she worked with was from a roll of bleached camel gut that the villagers typically kept for everyday use.

Carefully she drew the two sides of the cut together, moving along until it was fully closed. At the same time Tana lightly sponged the oozing blood away.

When Tecwwa was finished, thirty large stitches were in place. Taking a long length of six inch wide muslin the two women tightly strapped David around his torso to keep their handiwork as stable as possible. Gently they removed the leather wadding from his mouth.

There was a split moment as Tana took the older woman's hand. She knew that Tecwwa had never done something like this before. For them both it was a tension, an emotion of a new and different sort: to treat, to mend outside their knowledge and upbringing.

He rolled over, tried to stand, but found that he was so stiff. The strapping immobilised him from waist up. Even his arms were bound. David lay there, gathering his thoughts; remembered the start of the treatment and then all thereafter was blank.

The tautness between his shoulder blades throbbed with a pulsing pain. He tried to stand once again; a touch on his shoulder, an arm went around him and mindful of his injury, assisted him to sit upright.

The woman was still dressed in black. With a flick of her hand she pushed her head scarf away, revealing her face.

He was jolted by her beauty. In such circumstances it was almost too much to believe. She said nothing as his gaze took her in.

Her cheekbones looked to be of pure Moor origin. They were high with wide set dark eyes above them. Her lips were full, almost cupid-pouting, which she had appeared to coat in some clear glossy protective crème. Her nose aristocratically fine, ears small and finely set. Despite living in such a harsh and hot environment, her skin appeared dusky yet clear, untouched or damaged by the blistering sun. He could see that there were slight lines at her eyes and around her mouth, determining an age he thought between thirty five and forty.

A heavy intricate amulet hung from her neck. She was clearly Tuareg. He guessed or more perceived that she must be a descendant from the upper class, the original noble.

David did not know what to say. He uttered the only word in Tamacheq he knew, following it in French and English.

'*Tan-oo-mert, merci,* thank you.'

From her look she understood but said nothing. Then her lips widened into a small smile.

There was a long pause.

'You lie still. Five, six days.'

Her English was spoken so softly that at first David thought his ears were deceiving him.

'You speak English?'

'A little, yes.'

Astounded, David did not know what to say, but she in fact continued.

'In village where I school. Long time ago. There was teacher, American woman. Work for Peace Corp. I learn. From her. For two year.'

'What is your name? Do you mind if I ask?'

'I am Tecwwa,' with another hesitant shy smile.

'And I am David.'

There was something about this white man, this toubab.

His eyes seemed so clean. When he said thank you.

Their blueness looked at her with genuine integrity.

She had never been near a white man before now. She had only ever seen them from a distance, always from within the shelter of her hut. The man in front of her looked strong and calm and respectful.

Unlike the men she occasionally came into touch with. The Tuareg men were too proud, but now no longer able to temper their pride with the time-honoured traditions and old way of life. The Bella remained subservient, the Fulani too unkempt, scruffy in their nomadic ways. The Dogon people intriguingly different and insular.

Living without a man and outside the village community for all these years had made her naturally cautious, sometimes even afraid and insecure. The village people, and especially the women, allowed her to live nearby, but only because of her healing knowledge. She knew that without the women's influence, the local men would either subjugate or ostracize her completely.

She sat there with him. It was so still.

'What is it I should feel?' She thought to herself. 'This is a white man under my care.'

The man spoke again. 'All I can remember were your hands; they were so careful, so tender.'

'I am medicine woman. By touch,' she said simply.

'You are more than that,' the man said openly.

She looked at him intently. There was a flutter within her, an emotion, a feeling shaken. Something felt, it seemed so long ago. An attraction, a stimulus of something long missing in her life.

He spent the days resting as Tecwwa had instructed. Although after day two he started taking short walks around the village settlement.

What at first he took to be a Tuareg village was actually a far more complicated settlement. It seemed to be divided into various areas. On the slopes of the escarpment and higher up with the houses close knit, lived the Dogon. Out in the flatter areas were the few Tuareg. In close proximity to them were the subservient Bella. On the sandy plains further out roamed the more itinerant Fulani, with their large herds of cattle and goats. There were Bambara and even a few Songhaï people as well.

Nearly a full kilometre away and situated on a slight rise, Tecwwa's house was removed from them all. There were two small squarish adobe huts, one only half-built and without a roof. A large acacia near the doorway provided shade for her few animals.

Although Tecwwa had treated the wounded Tuareg man, David instructed Moussa to take him to the clinic in Douentza for further care. At the same time, more supplies could be obtained for the two of them, for when they continued their own journey. This took Moussa away for three days as well.

Tecwwa would visit David twice a day. In the mornings she and Tana would bring him hot water and a little food; flat bread, or *farni*, sometimes a portion of grilled chicken.

They would loosen the strapping and clean the rapidly healing wound. Then bind it all tight again.

Tecwwa's hands seemed to vibrate when they touched him, a stimulation of his skin and nerve-endings; an active physical enhancement to the rapidly healing cut.

In the early evenings Tecwwa always came to see him alone.

The evening meal she brought was more substantial, always two deep bowls, one on top of the other. The larger lower one would contain rice or millet, in the smaller bowl would be a soup stew made with chicken or goat meat. From the folds of her tunic would emerge little plastic packets filled with spices; some pepper and a mix of salt, ground sage leaves and dried onion powder.

There was also a bucket of water for David to wash his hands and face, both before and after eating. Tecwwa would do the same.

With the first dinner she provided only one plate. When he had finished eating she washed the plate and ate a little herself.

David waited until she had finished.

'Please eat with me next time.'

Concealing the pleasure of his request and her face betraying nothing, she replied with downcast eyes. 'Not our way, men eat first.'

The white man nodded understandingly. 'I know, but for me it would be an honour for you to join me.'

Tecwwa remained inscrutable. Her thoughts deep, remembering how her father used to treat her mother as an equal. Not like the tribal men here. This man seemed to be like her father.

But the next night there were two plates. She dished for him and then herself. Together they ate quietly as the evening turned cooler.

From the small fire David had made she drew a few lumps of charcoal. On a wire brazier she brewed strong sweet black Arabic tea. Straining the tea over and over until it was frothy and smooth, Tecwwa filled two small glasses. They drank it listening to the sounds; donkeys braying and goats bleating as the little village boys herded them home.

He gradually learned more of her background. Tecwwa's English was halting, slightly staccato, as she recalled words and phrases learnt long ago. Yet at the same time he found her voice to be dulcet and charming.

Of her family she told him only two things; David was careful not to pry any further.

Tecwwa's voice was neutral as she spoke. 'My husband dead many years ago, I have little information how.'

David looked into her eyes, sensing he should ask only one more question.

'And your parents?'

'From little girl, I learn from my mother. She good medicine woman. We collect plants and leaves and many things. She teach me.'

There was nothing more.

Every day they became more comfortable with each other; and the more she opened up, the more her true spirit began to emerge. Despite her difficult circumstances, she liked to be light-hearted and happy, helpful and cheerful.

And she was so understatedly alluring.

It was a time of indescribable pleasure for David, a future memory of moments of total peace.

As he would realise when later she spoke of it, it was a similar awareness for Tecwwa as well.

Even when Moussa returned, the equilibrium remained unchanged. Moussa stayed away at mealtimes. It was something he knew to be right.

At the end of those six days, the medicine woman and her helper cleaned the wound for the last time. Tecwwa showed Moussa how to remove the stitches if called upon to do so, telling him they had to be taken out in another few days.

A salve was produced for David to smear on for a while thereafter.

That last night there were little additional things David noticed when they shared the dinner she had prepared. Tecwwa wore a different robe, still black but with fine silver threadwork on the sleeves and at the neck. She had attended to her finger and toenails, cleaning and coating them carefully so that they gleamed in the firelight.

For the first time she totally removed the head scarf she normally wore. David saw that her hair was long, below her shoulders almost to waist level, jet-black and straight, washed, brushed through many times.

They drank the strong tea and talked, small segments of slightly broken conversation.

She stayed longer than normal.

'We leave tomorrow, I do not know what to do to or how thank you. Can I give you money? Or provisions?'

With her dark eyes glowing Tecwwa looked at him circumspectly, paused, before replying, 'I would like....please....one thing only.'

David said nothing.

'Come back. One time. Maybe more time. To see me.'

Chapter 6
Whitey

David could not be sure what his life would be like after leaving the mine. Having worked for so many years in regular employment brings a security; security of regular money, health care and housing. Roots become deep.

But now he was adrift. On his own.

He found that it was not as insecure as he thought.

The structure and discipline ingrained after so many years was still there. He budgeted carefully, paid the insurances, maintained his Land Rover properly and planned his trips and arrangements.

All this was done in the knowledge that it was for himself.

Moussa was his guide and driver and had become his friend, but, at the end of the day, there was still an employment contract with him to be honoured.

Now in the space of a week, after nearly three years on the road, a totally new dimension had entered David's life.

In a location so remote, in an environment so implacably harsh and unforgiving, there was a woman of indescribable appeal. A woman isolated, living almost as an outcast, who had made a request of him.

What appeared to be a simple entreaty, was in fact not. It was a request of such complexity. Nearly eight years of being alone, often lonely, was there now someone for him? Someone who would be more than a companion and more than a friend? A woman with whom to share life and love, a woman who wanted to become part of his future.

David was completely distracted.

For the next two days he let Moussa drive as they made their way slowly across Mali to the river town of Mopti. The gravel roads were in very poor condition. They could not afford for his perplexity to lead to a lack of concentration, to result in an accident or casualty.

They stopped in scruffy, raucous Mopti whilst David decided what to do next.

In the end it was Moussa who suggested that they go see Whitey and his wife. 'It is only one day away. You stay there for a while. I take holiday to Senegal then we can continue.'

Meeting up with Whitey and Marie le Roux again was, for everybody, a welcome change. With satellite TV and newspapers flown in, it was a chance for David to catch up on the wider world. And for the Le Rouxs, he was the fresh wind, away from "life on the mine."

Marie was an artistic French woman, chic and voluble, often bored with the regimen of ladies clubs, and tea and tennis parties.

For some reason she and Whitey had decided not to have children, which David thought, but never uttered, made their lives incomplete. Within him he sensed he knew the reason.

During the course of his military service with the South African Defence Force, Whitey had seen, and probably done, some terrible things. Once, in an unguarded moment and well into a second bottle of red wine, he and David shared anecdotes.

'You remember that incident with the crocodiles in the Caprivi?' David asked.

'Which one? There were a few.'

'You know when the soldiers wanted to swim in the Kavango River they used to throw hand grenades into the river to chase the crocs away.'

'Remind me.'

'Well, one Sunday afternoon this sapper throws the grenade in. Unfortunately six of his mates are already in the water. Kills four and severely wounds the other two.'

Whitey put his finger to his temple, 'Even now I can

remember his name. Van Schalkwyk, dumbest bloodly *troepie* I ever knew.'

And then he was off with a story of his own.

It was clearly one that he should never have told, should have kept buried deep within him; never to be repeated. But it was one Whitey found impossible to forget, and probably the reason that he refused to father children.

'About a year after you finished in the force, I was seconded to the *Koevoet* for six months.'

South Africa, and its defence of South West Africa/Namibia, did not capitulate militarily when it agreed to change. Change was brought about by economic and political sanction. Change was delivered by a white leader De Klerk and a black leader Mandela who both knew that another way to rule had to be found, otherwise Southern Africa would deflagrate.

Yet even at this time of change, South Africa's white led armed forces were virtually invincible. The South African Defence Force and its army in particular, still enjoyed support by large sectors of the population.

It was a motivated, well equipped and highly trained machine. At its elite end were special units, parabats and reconnaissance, the reccies. This was where Whitey and David served, David as a citizen force member, Whitey a permanent force platoon leader.

Surprisingly the police, independently of the SADF, had a special unit too.

This division was called *Koevoet*. A dreaded, infamous and at times notorious name.

Koevoet means crowbar.

The illustration was to prise open. Prise open information. Prise out terrorists, the so-called liberation fighters. Prise in any location sometimes deep into Angola. Prise under cover of the local population.

All *Koevoet's* leaders were highly intelligent and aggressive. And they were all volunteers; policemen who chose to police in another way.

The special constables were all volunteers too, but with them there was more to it. Most were former liberation fighters who had turned; turned away and disillusioned with their black political leaders in exile who they believed had let them down. These constables were equally well drilled, originally by Cuban, Russian and East German instructors; invariably trained in the most deprived and horrendous conditions.

They were ethnically local, now totally committed to *Koevoet* and its white group leaders.

Even by military counter-insurgency standards, *Koevoet* operated brazenly outside the norm.

Nine times out of ten, their missions were successful. They looked after the population and weeded out armed insurgents. Somehow over time and through their protective actions, they gained the confidence and co-operation of the local Ovambo tribe.

But the *Koevoet* unit that Whitey was seconded to as an intelligence officer was different. The man leading it was a non-smiling, cold as ice, sociopathic lieutenant; and his men were just like him.

'It was the worst fokken six months of my whole life. Those bastards had no respect or value for human life.'

David could recall the stress on Whitey's face as he spoke. When a hard, tough man flinches, it is usually from deep emotional misfortune and not physical adversity.

'We were chasing SWAPO insurgents, terrs, on the border between South West Africa; Namibia they call it now, and Angola. There was this Ovambo compound full of people.'

He drank deeply from his wine glass. '*Iechyd da*. Good Health.'

Then grimacing slightly, Whitey carried on, 'the *Koevoet* chased them all outside and made two lines. On one side are all the children up against the stockade. Nowhere to run. On the other side are all the men and women, even the old and weak who can just about stand.'

Whitey looked at his friend. 'The lieutenant, this hard case mad man from who knows where, someone not even his mother could love, starts to talk. He doesn't shout, doesn't give orders; just talks quietly. Just laid-back and placid. He speaks good Ovambo, with some Afrikaans thrown in. Anybody would think that it's just a little church meeting to discuss who carries the

48

fokken collection plates.'

For a few seconds there was total silence.

'This lieut takes out his firearm and shoots a small boy. Dead, one shot. The villagers start to make noise. His troops keep them in line. Very quietly he asks where the terrs are.'

Whitey shuddered, seemed to be reliving the horror all over again.

'The bastard shoots another child. This time in the neck. Blood everywhere. One of the women leaves her line. The *Koevoet* drag her back.'

'Whitey, you don't have to tell me the rest.'

'Ag, man, what the hell. He kills another one, a little girl, maybe two years old. One of the elders starts to shout. They club him down.'

David's friend sighed, looked at his now empty glass. 'It takes six children before they crack. Four or five of the women start to shout and point. There is a man in the line who tries to break for it. He doesn't get far. Another tries to sneak away, gets shot in the leg.'

Whitey's fierce eyes had that hollow, distant look. 'The women gave the terrs up, their own kind, probably family, to save their children.'

David studied his friend's face. 'That's not all, is it?'

'No,' Whitey sighed. 'That fokken lieutenant holds his hands up to quieten the bedlam. His troops smack a few more people around. Fire shots into the air. Then thoughtfully, very bloody thoughtfully, the bastard says that next time he asks a question they shouldn't take so long to answer.'

David thought that was the end of it, but Whitey went on. 'David, do you know what happened next?'

'No....but I can imagine. You don't have to tell me.'

'This maniac shoots all the women and children, one by one. Even in between, when he runs out of bullets, he looks around and slowly, very slowly reloads his pistol. When he's finished he goes up to an elder who appears to be the village chief. This time the bastard screams; DON'T TRY TO BREED.....OR LOOK AFTER TERRS HERE AGAIN.'

After that, David knew why Whitey couldn't face a child, look one in the eye, hold one in his lap. The memory would come back with every touch.

When one looked at Marie, one saw a woman seemingly out of place. She had grown up near Paris and was every part the modern Parisian woman.

Even living in a mining compound, in a remote and far-off location hadn't changed her. She and Whitey lived a life that was essentially French. The furnishings in their house were modern and imported. A few African artefacts were tastefully placed to soften the effect. Vogue and Elle magazines were on the side tables. Some of her own stylized landscape paintings hung from the walls.

The clothes she wore were chiffon-light, ordered by mail from the boutiques in France.

Their mealtimes were geared around a leisurely petit déjeuner in the mornings and a late slow evening meal.

At first one might wonder how she and Whitey connected, but they did and were surprisingly very happy together; they adored each other beyond question. Marie kept him in line with quiet, loving fortitude. And Whitey in turn had placed her on a worship pedestal, with an enjoyment and admiration she fully deserved.

David thought that she would not stay with him for long. But the second time he had dinner with them after taking the Mine Manager's position, she told him about their marriage.

'We were married just outside Paris near my home town of Orléans. Whitey brought his mother and father across and one of his friends, Piet de Beer, to be his best man. That is all. Me, I come from a large family so there are plenty of people from my side. Maybe two hundred! All of them, everyone, my parents and friends included say I am crazy to marry this man. It will never last. We are, what you say, incompatible. He is a wild man, an Afrikaner, a racist and a bigot.'

Marie smiled, 'but they do not know Whitey like I know him.'

'We have the church marriage and then a reception at a small chateau. Everything is very nice. But then it became wonderful.'

'What happened?' David asked.

'Whitey gets up to thank everybody. He even manages a little French. My people start to listen. I sense a change in the room. But then Whitey changes them completely and I know he will always be the man, the only man, for me.'

'Marie, what did he do?'

'David, he started to sing. Do you know that as a boy he was classical trained? Beautiful tenor voice. First he sings *Nkosi Sikelel' iAfrika*. Everybody applauds politely.'

Marie looked at her audience. 'What do you think Whitey did next?'

'I've no idea ... propose a toast?'

'Ooh, David, now I can see why everyone calls you clever. Yes, he propose a toast. In song. The beginning of Bizet's *Toreador*; it starts.

Your toast, I can give it to you

Melodiously she hummed the tune until,

it is the day of celebration

Hummed further,

Toreador, love, love awaits you!

'David, in mid-song Whitey changes. His technique is so good.'

'What did he sing next?'

'He goes straight into Donizetti's *Malatesta*. Beautiful aria. Do you know it?'

'No.'

She recited a verse for him,

Lovely as an angel
come down on earth
fresh as the lily
that opens at dawn;
eyes that speak and laugh,
a look that wins the heart,
hair darker than ebony,
an enchanting smile.

'When he is finished, there is at first silence, then the room, the guests go mad. They clap and clap and clap. Many are crying, even the men. Ah, the French men,' and she laughed.

'The people come up to the table where we are sitting. They hug and kiss him over and over. They do the same to me.

By singing of his love for me, brings their acceptance. I am so happy. Even now after six years of marriage, whenever we visit France, the people always ask him to sing.

They know now why Whitey is my man'.

David stayed with the Le Rouxs while Moussa took his holiday. The doctor who worked at the mine took a look at his back and removed the stitches.

'Couldn't have done a much better job myself,' he said. 'Would have used a thinner thread, maybe a few more stitches, but otherwise everything is fine. The skin is healing nicely. What have you been using?'

'I've no idea,' David replied.

He showed him the salve Tecwwa had given him.

The doctor smelt it. 'There's something slightly aromatic, vanilla myrrh or something. Seems to have worked really well. Where did you get it?'

'From the person who did the stitches.'

'Is he a traditional healer?'

'No, it's a she. A Tuareg, they call her a medicine woman.'

The man's eyebrows rose in surprise, but that was how the discussion ended.

Whitey le Roux was a man of such depth that David believed it was only Marie and himself who knew what made him function. Whitey's upbringing had shaped him, made him resilient and resourceful, physically hardened.

The family farm was in south western Namibia, bordering on the Sperrgebiet diamond concession areas. It was an immense holding: over thirty five thousand hectares of semi-arid land. There were large herds of karakul sheep ideally suited to the terrain and environment. In some areas were pockets of game, a few ostriches and, surprisingly, feral horses. Namibia had originally been a German colony. When it surrendered towards the end of World War One, the Germans' horses were turned loose. Now they bred and ran wild.

Whitey's childhood was difficult. His Afrikaans father was a difficult and embittered ex-miner, his mother an unyielding woman from the Welsh valleys who regretted marriage from the day she fell pregnant.

The farmworkers brought him up. In fact, his father treated him like a worker too. Whitey herded sheep and mended fences. Boreholes were re-piped and their pumps repaired. Many long nights were spent out in the veld sleeping on cold hard ground.

From somewhere he received a rudimentary education; this improved during his fifteen year military service. His mother only really gave him one thing. She taught Whitey to sing. Celtic songs of praise, folk songs in Welsh; French and Italian operatic arias and serenades.

And Whitey could sing. When he opened his mouth in song, a sound emerged, sweet and mellifluous, sweet yet powerful, the tenor controlled and fluent.

His devotion to Marie and David was total. And, to be fair, so was theirs to him.

In the apartheid-era South Africa, all white boys leaving school were conscripted in the South African Defence Force. One might defer serving by going to university first, but it could never be avoided. They were the citizen force and served compulsory periods ranging from nine months to two years.

David's introduction to Whitey was straightforward.

'Hey, you, lower-than-dog-shit. Stand up straight otherwise I'll push this baton through your ears and ride you like a Harley Davidson.'

He was the most demanding and ferocious Permanent Force drill sergeant in the training period.

After two months of training hell they were posted into different units. David was assigned to a border reconnaissance patrol where Whitey, newly elevated to platoon leader, arrived two weeks later to take control.

When he first saw David again, there was an immediate explosive reaction. *'Bliksem*, you again! It took me months to teach you to march, how long is it now going to take to teach you to track! Fokken hell!'

But slowly his exasperation swung to grudging respect.

The recruiting and distribution officers in the South African Defence Force generally managed to place the citizen force in appropriate divisions. Those mechanically inclined landed up in vehicle maintenance; farm boys who could shoot, really shoot, became snipers, others who could type became signallers.

David was comfortable in the bush. This knowledge landed him in a reconnaissance unit. He could read animal tracks, make a fire without matches, live off the land; knew the edible berries and how to find water in very dry conditions.

Whitey was a disciplinarian through and through. His missions were planned with total meticulousness. Within the given intelligence he left nothing to chance. The men seconded to him were like his children. During the eighteen months David served under him, he never lost a man, never had a fatality.

When one of the units suffered a casualty he would make them analyse the situation over and over again.

'Troepies,' he would say, 'I do not want to lose one of you and you, sure as hell do not want to lose me.'

He drove a loyalty and tightness into the unit that made the commanding officers take notice. They were given difficult and complex tasks; scouting missions on foot deep into Angola and Zambia. Whitey received rapid promotions.

The day David finished his military service, Whitey came up to him and shook his hand. The first time he had ever done so.

'David,' also a first. 'I am proud to have served with you.'

With that he saluted and turned away. David thought that he would never see him again.

Now the two men sat there on the patio. Moussa had arrived back and it was time to travel on.

As was his way, Whitey made David go over the weapons and drug running that he had seen in the escarpment. He made careful notes and plotted the exact location, sketched the possible routes. David had to describe the guns in as much detail as he could remember.

'You never know when this will be useful. There are more and more reports of this kind. Bandit groups are also starting up, especially in the very remote areas. It's easier for them to rob and steal than to work honestly. Kidnapping too.'

Then he changed track.

'David, I'm glad we've seen you again. But you seem a wee bit agitated, *ffrind*.' The Welsh creeping in as it sometimes did.

'Yes, it's true. And it's a little complicated.'

'Marie thinks there's a woman involved.' His pale eyes gleamed with a slight mischief.

'Yes, she's right. But I don't know what to do.'

'The woman's married?'

'No, no, at least I don't think so. Not anymore,' David replied.

Whitey looked at him questioningly.

'Her husband was killed in the Tuareg rebellion. Years ago. You see, she's a Tuareg.'

'Fokken hell, David. A black nomad. A camel follower!'

'Take it easy Whitey. She lives near a Dogon village, permanently. Treated my back.'

'She a witchdoctor?' And he laughed loudly, threw his arm around David. 'Boy, she must be something to have you looking, have you confused.'

He laughed again.

'Look David, you can do no worse than me. I married a French woman, and her sister; and her mother and her grandmother and even some of Marie's ugly girlfriends.

Sometimes being a continent away is not far enough! Still too close!'

He looked at his friend, then said quietly, 'I'm sorry. Ignore what I said. After all those years in the army and everything that went with it, I still met Marie, my precious lady. You deserve someone. Let us meet her soon.'

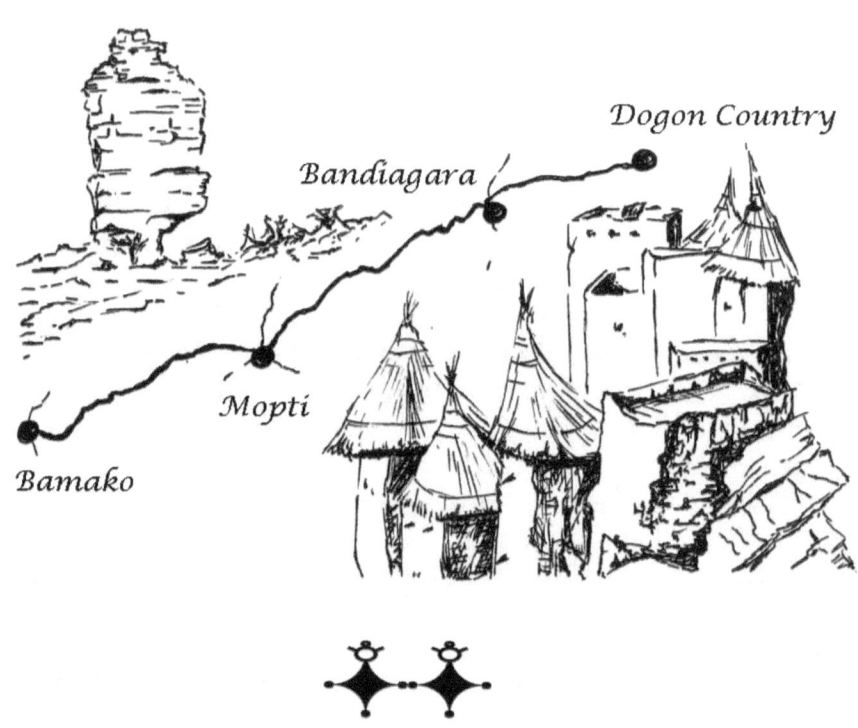

Chapter 7
Return

From Bamako, David and Moussa headed east towards Burkina Faso in an anti-clockwise circle. The plan was to visit the Nassoumfou area and search for some of the desert elephant that roamed there.

They weren't quite sure where they were, but knew that tracking them in a northerly direction would bring them back up into Mali. And not far from Tecwwa.

It was tough going. They found a small group moving quickly north. There had been a lot of rain in the area and the normally dry watercourses were filled with water and very muddy patches. For the Sahel the humidity was oppressive. The men drank plenty of water, but still remained ever thirsty and dehydrated.

During the heat of the day they would observe the elephants resting in the shade; a few would browse for the choicest leaves, the others dozing on their feet. Overnight they would be gone, the next day already forty kilometres away. It was difficult to even tell how many animals there were.

They kept following them until the border into Mali was crossed; then turned north-west away from the elephants and motored towards the nearest point of the Bandiagara escarpment. The two men had been in the bush for nearly four weeks and their supplies were very low. By now they were also less than fifty kilometres from Tecwwa's village. There they would be able to re-stock and rest.

Counting the time David had spent with Whitey and Marie, almost two months had passed since Tecwwa had uttered those words, *Come back. One time. Maybe more time. To see me.*

They had gone through his mind over and over.

A woman like Tecwwa only says the things she means. There is no frivolity. Life was too strenuous and difficult. Existence for a single woman living in a desert village was a hardship that many would not be able to comprehend.

Now David was back. And wanted to be there.

Slowly Moussa drove up the desert track and into view of the settlement. And gradually, as they approached, an excitement of joy and expectation struck David. He really wanted to see her again.

He turned to Moussa. 'We'll go to her hut first. I need to greet her.'

Moussa just smiled.

She was standing in her doorway.

'So soon,' she whispered, 'so soon.' Almost an assertion to herself that David had really returned.

'Yes.'

He held out his hand. Tecwwa took it in both of hers and for a brief moment touched it to her cheek.

'I need to find a place for Moussa to stay. And for myself, please. And we need to wash. We are both very dirty. As you can see.'

Without hesitation she asserted, 'You stay. Here.'

To her great excitement, for she had never been in a motor vehicle before, her helper Tana went with Moussa to the village to arrange some lodgings for him.

At the back of Tecwwa's house was an outbuilding of sorts, a half-built mud shanty divided into two. One part was a pit toilet, the other had buckets of water neatly placed in line on the floor. A broken mirror hung on the wall. A low shelf held scraps of soap and an almost empty bottle of shampoo. That was all.

While washing, David could hear Tecwwa bustling around preparing food and tea.

As he finished he saw her climb a ladder up onto the flat roof of her little house. With a grass hand broom she swept the roof and placed a sleeping mat down for him.

Tana came rushing back. She brought bread and fruit, a few small sunburned bananas and mangoes, and in a plastic packet, diced pieces of meat. With a happy flourish, she handed everything over to Tecwwa.

Tana was so elated; smiling and laughing, chattering continually to Tecwwa who had no chance to reply, or even get a word in.

David couldn't follow a word but imagined the gist of it all.

The white man had come back to see Tecwwa! There must be gifts! She, Tana had been in a motor car! She, Tana, was going to see her friends in the next village. Moussa was going to take her! She, Tana, thought Moussa was so handsome, so tall, so clever with languages! She, Tana, knew there were joyous times ahead!

Moussa arrived looking clean and refreshed. With a wave to his friend he bustled Tana into the Land Rover. Her continued animation was audible even as they drove away.

Tecwwa and David were alone.

'I go wash, before we eat,' she said.

He sat there waiting for her. Tecwwa's evident pleasure at his return brought contentment, a subtle tranquillity.

Again she had taken care to dress and beautify. Connecting and through her eyebrows, an artistically shaped line had been drawn in kohl. A little silver glitter dust had been brushed into her hair, which shimmered in the candlelight as they ate.

Tecwwa was stunning. On first appearance normally so quiet and serious, now she was relaxed, more carefree. David laughed as she re-told Tana's exuberant utterances. It was just as he had thought.

In halting English she also told him of the happenings in the village. He asked her about the gun runner.

'He get better, but take more time. I help him. Rub broken muscles.'

'And the guns?'

'Men of village find. Send on. They grateful to you. You safe in this area.'

'What do you mean by safe?'

'In other places, white people not safe. Bad men there.'

Whiteys' comments rang a bell. If in the future, David wanted to travel deeper into eastern Mali with Moussa, they would definitely need to get more information first.

The next few days unfolded at a gentle pace.

There was much in the surrounding Dogon area to see and explore. In the higher, difficult to access reaches of the Falaise, tiny animistic settlements maintained a lifestyle that was over five hundred years old. The people followed paganistic beliefs: strangely daubed, fetish temple sites were decorated with peculiar signs and symbols. Nailed to the rock walls were dog and monkey skulls, and the skins of large rodents and snakes hung over openings.

In the evenings when they ate together, Tecwwa told David more of these unusual Dogon people. She asked for his notebook and made simple drawings to illustrate what she was saying.

'The elders, the men have special meeting place, always with nine pillars. It is called,' and she printed the word TOGU-NA, 'you cannot go in there, you have to be invited.'

She explained how the mud tombs were made, high up on the almost sheer precipices, 'and when Dogon woman die, her sleeping mat and millet-pounding pot is left with her body there.'

'And this is granary for man in afterlife,' she traced an outline for David to look at, 'it has millet. The granary for woman is smaller, because no millet allowed.'

David enjoyed listening to her talk. Every day he learned a little more of her.

That she was tough and resourceful was without doubt. With perfect posture and balance she could carry 25 litres of water on her head from the well to her hut. At the same time there would be a load of firewood tied to her back. A goat could be killed, skinned and cut up within half an hour. Whatever she did seemed always to be with decorum and graceful strength.

Underlying it all was a probing intelligence, though somewhat stifled by living where she had for so long. Her education too was better than expected. She read whatever literature she could get her hands on, whether in Tamacheq, Arabic, French or English.

From his pocket David took out a gift and offered it to Tecwwa.

'I have brought this for you, I hope you like it.'

She looked at him thoughtfully. 'If I take, you know what this mean?'

'Yes, I think so, but I'm not sure, not certain,' he replied.

'In our culture it mean you make claim. Make claim on me.'

He nodded.

Tecwwa's eyes seemed to blacken. David couldn't tell whether it was from fear or anger. Or something else.

'You have woman, have wife?' she queried.

'No, I have no one.'

In that lowly room with the candle lambent, he could feel the tension building. She looked down, obviously considering what to say next.

Time seemed to stretch. Then Tecwwa did a surprising thing. She stood, pulled the hood down over her head and went out into the night. Left him alone.

About ten minutes later she returned.

She called from outside and David went to her.

In her arms she held a baby goat. A tiny kid probably a week old. Almost formally she handed her gift to David, and led him back into her home.

Slowly she unwrapped the present he had given her, and gasped in amazement when it lay in her hand. The bracelet was finely filigreed, pure silver. In the middle, at its centre and in a solid gold inlay was an intricate circle of amber and turquoise surrounding polished iridescent agates and garnets.

Tecwwa admired it carefully, looked at David, spoke softly, slightly subdued.

'Your gift very...' struggling to find the right words, '...big cost. My gift so small.'

Saying nothing but still with the little goat in his lap he took her arm and fastened the bracelet to her left wrist. Bending forward Tecwwa lifted her face and drew him towards her. Their tongues just tipping, they shared a first kiss that was thrilling and heart-felt.

They sat there together, that fourth night of his return, holding hands, saying nothing. Just being together. A middle-aged man and middle-aged woman falling in love. Two people from totally different backgrounds and cultures finding each other.

David understood then, and it was an image that he would always and forever remember; when her eyes darkened, became nigrescent, it was a sign of desire and love and passion.

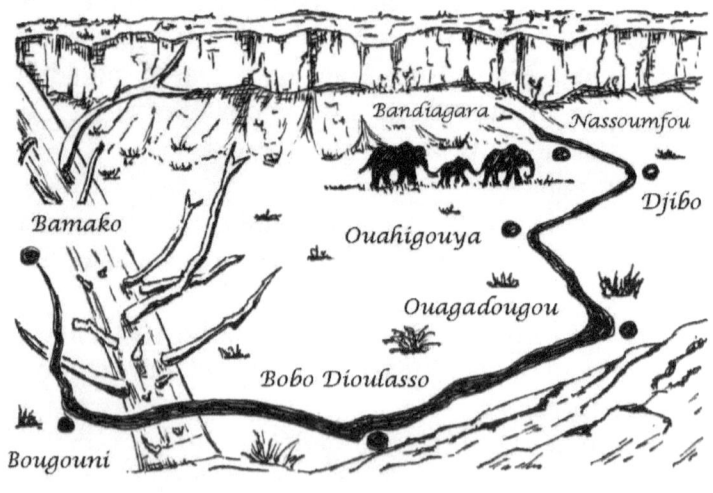

Chapter 8
Earthshine

David was settling down to sleep when he heard a soft footfall, heard the rickety ladder creak. For a moment he was wary and alert. Supporting himself on his elbow he reached for his knife.

The dark figure climbed over the parapet, moved toward him and knelt down, not saying anything.

Tecwwa studied him. In the slivered moonlight her look was profound and arcane. The moment was absolute and pure.

Quickly she slipped under the mosquito net. David helped her into his sleeping bag, unzipping it further to form a blanket over them.

Despite the evening being warm, Tecwwa was shivering.

'Hold me,' she murmured.

For a long while he held and stroked her until she slept. Through her clothes she felt lean and strong. A discreet fragrance contrasted her strength, a subtleness of something like roses, attar, an aromatic oil she was wearing. Tecwwa nestled in his arms, her features serene and tranquil.

David listened to the few night sounds. When the shrill clamour of the cicada died down another low repeated call took over. *Churr, churr, churr*, rapidly, over and over again.

'Must be one of the nightjars,' he thought to himself drowsily.

When David awoke it was just getting light; the white-pastel moon waning low in the west. The stars seemed so near, so clear in the desert night. Tecwwa was also awake.

He drew her close. The early dawn air was scented and cool.

'Always when I see the dark side of a crescent moon,' she whispered, 'I dream to have a man again.'

'Earthshine,' David said, and kissed her forehead.
'What?'
'When the moon glows like that, it is called earthshine.'

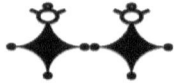

Chapter 9
Falcon

Those first days back with Tecwwa opened David's eyes to the harshness of her life; and to the difficulties facing the local village. The well was some distance away. Only the women, Tecwwa included, fetched water, carried in large drums on their heads.

She told him that in dry times the water table was very low. Self controlled rationing would then be implemented.

There was no infrastructure of any kind. There was no school. There was no money. All trade took place by barter or gift; favours to be returned when times got better. Tecwwa was as poor as everyone else.

David's return had sparked a great deal of curiosity too. Singly and in pairs the village women visited Tecwwa on the pretext of some minor ailment or malady. There could be no doubt that the couple were providing plenty of fuel for discussion and gossip.

But no-one was impolite or unfriendly. Wherever David walked, there were amiable greetings and gestures.

Tecwwa suggested a way to make it easier as well. She gave him a small bag of nuts; they looked like chestnuts.

'These are kola nuts,' she said. 'Take them with you when you walk around. When you hike in mountain. If you meet a man or woman who is more old, give one.'

'I have heard of these before,' David remarked.

'The old people like to chew kola,' Tecwwa went on, 'good for plenty things. For many illness. Like for sore head. Like for stomach not well. For joints that not move properly. Even,' and she smiled coyly, 'even to make strength for love.'

What David found was that the giving of these nuts showed respect and trust. And the receiving brought protection and support. The elders were always gracious and helpful whenever he dished them out.

Because Tecwwa had lived outside the village and been single for so long, the men also had no demand on her. She had remained aloof and unresponsive to them ever since the loss of her husband more than twenty years ago. Her obvious noble ancestry formed a natural taboo, as well.

Tana helped, too. Born locally, she had initially befriended Tecwwa to learn from her, to understand Tecwwa's medicinal skills. Now she was more than that; she was Tecwwa's helper, supporter and friend. And to some degree a protector as well.

Tana could be flighty, but she was devoted and sincere.

David had to be careful how he helped her. Resentment is easily caused in simple uneducated people. The last thing he wanted was for Tecwwa to be shunned by the community she had been part of, even though for all her time there, it had been a life slightly removed.

They spoke about this carefully. Their first decision was to help the village as a whole. Something everyone could benefit from, and, of course, Tecwwa too. First an improved water supply followed possibly by a small, single class-roomed school.

With permission and guidance from the village elders, they identified a site for a second well. Though slightly further away, an alternate source of water was seen as vital.

Through his past mining contacts, David arranged, and paid for a drilling contractor to sink a borehole, properly sleeved, substantially below the normal water table. The contractor donated a hand operated pump which David and Moussa mounted securely on a concrete base. Leading to one side they built a long concrete trough which would take any overspill; a source for the livestock to use.

They taught two of the local men how to do the basic maintenance; bolts that occasionally needed tightening and joints greased.

A celebration party took place when the new well was commissioned. Government officials came from Sèvarè to thank them. But for David there were two things of greater importance. The local people now used this water; the old well, with its buckets and ropes, kept in reserve.

More notably, however, he sensed that Tecwwa had gained. The respect for her medicinal ability was one thing; this was something else.

She could have chosen for him to help her first; instead, she chose to help the community.

The officials made their speeches, but the villagers' eyes looked at the woman standing slightly behind David. There was no jealousy or animosity; there was only a display of reverence, and an obeisance to her that made him proud.

He had also been unnecessarily worried about their cohabitation, whether it was perceived to be immoral or wrong. Now his fears were stilled.

They left the festivities to continue without them and walked slowly towards Tecwwa's house.

The escarpment, with its huge boulders copper burnished in the afternoon sun threw long shadows down.

About half way back she stopped, put her hand on David's arm, then through to hold it tightly. A gesture so open, so unusual, for a moment he was nonplussed. There was more. Slowly she removed her head scarf, her hair black gleaming ebony.

Looking intensely at him, Tecwwa spoke. 'Please. Never to leave me. My David, please. You are my love.'

Her eyes searched his face. This beautiful solitary desert woman who had been alone so long.

For a moment, emotion choked him. He almost could not speak.

'I am yours,' he breathed. 'You are my love too.'

'Come. To follow me,' Tecwwa turned away.

A narrow passage, one that David had never noticed before, led through the rocks and boulders. At places it was just wide enough for a single person to pass. Above, the tall cliffs arched to close over them.

Slowly they wound along the path, steadily climbing up the mountainside.

Suddenly there was a gaping chasm in front of them, about ten feet wide, to where the trail resumed on the other side.

'How do we get across? It's too far to jump,' David said.

Tecwwa pointed to two large logs, each with an attached length of rope, standing propped on their side of the rift.

'I show you.'

He could see how they formed a narrow draw bridge. There were four rebates chiselled in the solid rock and into these, the logs neatly fitted. They lowered them carefully into position making sure they were securely placed. Cautiously they crossed to the other side.

Wending their way along David became aware of the sound of water, the noise increasing with every step they took. Around the next bend from beyond and high above them, a slender plume of water fell into a crystal clear tarn.

In the reflecting sunlight, it was a lovely place. The wild grass was green and verdant. Small pretty red-throated bee-eaters flitted around, catching insects in swoops across the water surface. High up at the top of a cliff, a large bird perched. When it called, a chopping "*kak-kak-kak*", David thought it to be a

Lanner Falcon, surely a fitting place for a scarce, uncommon bird.

Knowing they were alone and not even looking around, Tecwwa unfurled her headscarf, slipped off her robe and removed her underwear. With a tentative step she put her left foot into the water. Slowly she went in until waist deep.

There had been no attempt to conceal herself, or any false modesty. Tecwwa stood there nude and David's eyes took her in. The skin on her upper body and stomach so smooth and lustrous; nipples black and aroused on her aureate breasts.

And now he could also see the underlying strength. The muscles of her arms, shoulders and legs were tightly shaped and sinew tough, testament to the many years of unceasing hard work and an arduous lifestyle.

David knew then what she was saying to him, saying without words, offering. She was giving him herself. Everything of her: open in the sunlight, with nothing to be concealed or hidden. Not just her physical attributes, not her few possessions or her way of life. She was doing something that would never be taken back. It was an award of her whole entity, for him to accept and share.

He was entrusted to be her man; the one she wanted to live and be with for the remainder of her life.

David felt still, almost stunned, as if he had stopped breathing. His mind so absorbed; his inner spirit, working with this emotional information, seemed to hold him back, appear withdrawn.

As if from a great distance Tecwwa called to him. 'Come, my David, come to water.'

Going over to the little lake, he, as she had done, removed all his clothes. Warmed by the sun, the shallow water was surprisingly temperate. Tecwwa sat in his encircling arms, her back tight to his chest. Gently, David cupped her breasts. Leaning back, she stretched up to kiss him lightly.

Her face was so lovely, peace and contentment smoothing the tiny age-lines, peace and contentment mirrored by the surroundings.

Minutes passed. Contemplative almost meditating, with her eyes half closed, Tecwwa began humming; a low vibrating strain, melodic and repetitive.

Later on, when David knew more of her and the Tuareg culture, he would recognise it as a contralto song of love and praise.

A woman in love and in praise of her man.

This man is doing so much for me.

After all these years it is as if I have value again. A value for myself and a value to others. Something that is more than just for my medicine and massage.

All this time I barely existed, living only from one day to another. Sometimes in the summer drought, so poor, that it was from one small meal a day to one small meal the next day. Those first years were so difficult. The anguish and loneliness should have destroyed me.

How did I survive?

Now I have a man again. How does this destiny work?

My grandmother used to say that the big falcon is a messenger. They fly high and from far and because they are seldom seen, the messages they bring are so important. The falcon up on the mountainside must have first brought David to me. And then told him to return to Tecwwa.

The bird and earthshine must be connected, linked to bring me happiness again.

My David is a white man but he treats me like an equal, talks to me like an equal. Why should I find this so surprising? Is it because my father did not, my husband did not, my teachers, even the American woman, did not?

He listens: no, it is more than that. He reveres me with patience and love.

And he desires me. It is like a bull. I can feel his hard sex tight up against my back as we sit here together.

And I want him. I am ready now for my David. I am ready to receive a man again. I am so warm and soft inside. Tonight we shall join together. Time has come to give him everything of me.

The bird and earthshine have to be linked, to bring me such happiness again.

Chapter 10
Stillbirth

The vastness of the night sky glowed, illuminated by the full moon's light. It was so bright that they could see down to the village, and even further; over across the small hillocks towards the sandy plains. Next to the doorway, the branches of the large tree cast clear-silhouetted penumbrae; contrasting strong shadows of grey and black.

They sat close together, not quite touching. Hesitantly Tecwwa talked to David, slowly opening the portal to her early life. He tried not to interrupt or ask questions, just let her reminisce; find her own way back to her youth.

Her Tuareg upbringing was so protected; womenfolk kept well away from any possible indiscretion. An ill-considered conversation with a boy, a careless contact, could lead to being put to death.

'I was allocated to my cousin for marriage,' she explained. 'Very young.... I was not yet woman. So I still live with my mother. Still go to school.'

Her look to David was uncertain; a wavering, almost a fear of what she wanted to tell him.

'Our fore-fathers were Ihaggaren. My father and all his fathers were leaders. For the trade, with the camels. There is word, I am not sure.'

'Caravans?' David suggested.

'Yes, yes, that is word.'

She made as if to take his hand, but then pulled back.

'When I sixteen years, my father and mother let us marry. But my husband not happy, he not settle. Want to fight in war against Mali government.'

There had been Tuareg rebellions against authority going back to the early 1960s. Unhappy with a curtailment of their nomadic lifestyle and with deep suspicions that their culture was under threat, the Tuareg embarked on hit and run campaigns against state targets.

By 1965 these uprisings were quelled. But the problems and unease remained only to resurface in another insurrection in 1990.

Around this time Tecwwa's father and her husband decided that their womenfolk should be moved more south west, away from the fighting and danger.

'Many days we walk from east. Till we come here.'

'Where did you come from?' David asked.

'From Adrar des Ifôghas, from mountain.'

'And why did you come here?'

'My husband, his brother live here with Bella woman.'

Her voice could not disguise the inference. A Tuareg of noble lineage living with, what, until recent times, would have been one of their slaves.

'What happened next?'

'Nobody here. Brother and his woman gone. This was his house. Empty.'

A soft breeze blew. It flickered the candlelight, floating her delicate perfume across to David from where she sat on the other side of the floor mat. A smell of jasmine that would come to him later when he suffered so in captivity.

'My mother and sister refuse to live here. Near this village. They scared of Dogon people. But me, I have no choice. Must stay.'

'Why?'

'My husband say. Also I sick. Very.'

She paused, sighing sadly, gathering her thoughts, pulling at time-worn memories. By David's reckoning she had been here nineteen years on her own: the memories were likely to be difficult.

'Go on,' he said, moving closer, holding out his hand to her, 'share that time, that....hardship with me.'

She grasped his hand and her eyes filled with tears.

'My father pay for local woman to look after me. Also he give some goats and one camel. Then they leave to go back to mountain, back to Adrar.'

'Left you alone?'

'Yes, you see I with baby, longer than eight months. I can no more walk. Something also not right. Inside me. But I tell no one.'

'Not even your mother?'

'No,' she whimpered. 'My mother just want to leave this place.'

David leaned across and kissed her softly, tasted the salt of her tears. 'Carry on.'

'The local woman only bring me food and water. All other time I by myself.'

'And baby?'

'Oh David,' Tecwwa wept openly. 'Baby born dead.'

He held her tightly.

'I alone all the time. It was so bad. So much blood. I sick, sometime I think I almost dead.'

Tecwwa looked up. Her face was flooded with recollected torment.

'Somehow I cut cord. Try to clean. Inside me, much ...,' trying to find the right word '....damage, things torn. I try to fix a little. Like with you, with needle and gut.'

David's mind reeled. The image of what she was saying seemed so graphic. Delivering her own dead child, being her own midwife and surgeon. Stitching her ruptured vagina, her innermost tender flesh. But most of all, the pain. The physical agony must have been excruciating, but how had Tecwwa managed to survive the all-consuming, overwhelming grief. How mentally tough she had to have been.

'After some days when I stronger, I tie baby in goatskin and bury under rocks. Not far from this house.'

'What about the local people? Did they not help you?'

'No, they just leave me.'

The sympathy and concern on David's face must have been

74

evident. It seemed to calm Tecwwa a little. Her strong hands held him as if never to let go.

'Were the Dogon people not curious to know what happened?'

Tecwwa shook her head. 'These people are very different. Their ways very different. They see some things as punishment. Sometime, if family does very wrong, new baby killed.'

'They sacrifice children?'

'Yes, David, the Dogon have places, like temple, where they do these things.'

'So they left you alone.'

'Yes, they not sure what happened. I think then they scared of me. Now is different.'

For a while they sat there. Eventually, David gently loosened her grip and stood up. Moving to the shelf he fetched the tea. From the small fire outside he placed burning charcoal into the brazier. Quickly Tecwwa took over.

'You don't trust my tea making,' David teased gently.

There was a little smile back. Something seemed to have lifted from her. He realised then what it was; 'Tecwwa, I do not want to upset you anymore, but can I.....'

She interrupted before he could finish, 'I know what you want to ask. I have never before told anyone. No-one. What happened. Not till you today. And,' she wiped a tear away with her sleeve, 'I have never seen or heard from my family again. One time my husband brother's wife came here. Long time ago. She tell me my husband dead, killed in fighting. Of my father, mother and sister she know nothing.'

David went over to her and held her again. 'You have been in pain and very sad for a long time, my darling.'

'You came back to me, my David. Now you are healing me.'

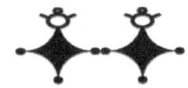

PART 2

SEPARATION

Chapter 11
Shadows

What information they had was so minimal. The location of the settlement they were looking for seemed unknown to all. Everyone David and Moussa spoke to just shook their heads. A suggestion was even made that the place could be in Algeria.

Eventually a Bambara man came forward who had something to say. 'I think that it is not just a village. It is also a valley deep in the Adrar.'

Tecwwa's memory had to have faded in time. As a child and young woman she led a sheltered life within a nomadic family, where mainly the men trekked. The women almost always stayed behind. Her geographic knowledge was limited only to a description of the immediate physical location, and, more broadly, that it was in the east. How to get there, or back, was beyond her recall.

Even the people David and Moussa asked now looked sceptical.

'Why are you looking for that place?' one of them questioned.

Moussa launched into an explanation of a Tuareg family which had gone west many years ago, and that some of them had returned soon after.

'Now the ones still living in the west, near Dogon, are looking for the ones who returned to the east, to Adrar des Ifôghas.'

The Bambara man spoke again. 'You could ask the Tuareg here, maybe some of them know. If they will talk to you.'

'Why *if?*' Moussa queried.

'They don't like to talk about the old times, about the old

ways,' the Bambara said enigmatically.

But David knew what he meant. When you take a nomadic people's freedom away, when you curtail them to boundaries, to borders that have never been, force their lives into a direction often ill-thought out, you create suppression. Suppressed people are difficult, do not like to talk.

They spent another unsuccessful day in Kidal but still found no-one who could help them. Late that afternoon, as they were loading the vehicle to make the long journey home, an elderly Tuareg man leading a few camels passed by.

'Speak to him. If he knows nothing that's it. We're on our way back tomorrow.'

In halting yet understandable Tamacheq, Moussa greeted the Tuareg.

The man stopped, clearly surprised, curiosity kindled. Once again Moussa explained what he and David were looking for.

Looking at them, he wrapped his indigo turban neatly around his face before responding. 'That was long ago, the time we wanted to fight. The government wanted us to become farmers, to live in the towns,' he said derisively, 'we should have fought more. At least I have my camels; others of our people are now peanut growers and shopkeepers.'

His attitude and bearing, his direct gaze, reminded David of the Masai living on the great plains of eastern Africa. The Masai, like this old Tuareg, feared and, for the most part, tolerated no-one.

He spoke again, 'this place you are looking for; only one road and one track!'

'Can we get there by car?' Moussa enquired.

The Tuareg sounded doubtful. 'Maybe some of the way. It is many years since I have been in that place.'

'Ask him if he will go with us,' David intervened. 'I will pay him for his help.'

But the elderly man declined bluntly. 'Who will look after my animals?'

The directions they received were given in camel-time.

One day to the north; a track to the right, in line with a high almost square mountain buttress; three more days travelling;

passing to the left side of the buttress would bring them to a valley entrance.

'The clan you are talking about came from those mountains. They were high people, Ihaggaren.'

'High people?' David questioned.

'He means noble people, chieftains,' Moussa replied.

'Ihaggaren? Could they be the same,' David pondered. 'Tecwwa said her ancestors were Ihaggaren.'

The Tuareg prepared to move on, pulled his camels into line.

'Moussa, what about the other track?'

'He says it starts in the same place then veers even more right through tight gorges. Only camels or people on foot can get through.'

The Tuareg looked at them, spoke to Moussa again. 'If you go, you must be careful. In the old days only good people, true people lived in the Adrar. These days it is not so.'

They were deep into the *massif* and the track was getting narrower and narrower.

What had originally been an old gravel road was now disintegrated into two thin stony abrasive lines. There was no evidence of the route being recently used; from appearances, not for years. Burnt yellow by the sun, knee-high grass grew concealing the track for short distances. Every so often David would have to scout ahead on foot looking for the way.

Moussa was clearly becoming more and more worried, 'Boss, I think we should turn around.'

David looked at his GPS and referred to the map.

'I think we're on the second road the man mentioned. Seems to be heading for those big sandstone hills.'

His friend and driver kept looking in his mirrors, continually turning to look back; as if he thought something or someone was pursuing them.

'We'll drive for another half hour or until the track finally disappears. Then turn around, whichever comes first.'

Slowly they pushed on. Moussa's unease was increasingly infectious. Even David, whose demeanour tended to be steadfast and calm, felt the affect. There was a moment when he thought he saw something far-off; a movement, perhaps an animal, a camel or gazelle. Then possibly a glint or reflection.

'Boss, I don't like this place!'

David did not reply. He could not see an obvious reason for concern, but now he was becoming edgy too. The terrain was harsh and unforgiving, but the two of them had been in places like this before. At least six hours of daylight remained. Providing they did not have a breakdown there was more than enough time to get back to the main road. Unusually for this time of year the heat was bearable; a slight breeze filtered through the outcrops.

Fifteen minutes later the track ran out altogether. There had probably once been a single-line path leading down a bumpy, rocky gulch. The boulders were large, up to five or six foot high, some even bigger; they were at a dead end and could go no further.

'Moussa, reverse slowly and I'll show you where to turn around.'

Even now that they were on the way back, his driver was still not happy. Moussa gradually began to speed up. The Land Rover jolted from side to side, thorn bushes scratching the sides of the car as they lurched along unsafely.

'Slow down, Moussa!'

There was a jarring thump as the underside of the front axle slid over a solid stone outcrop.

'Slow down, my friend,' David's patience was getting stretched as he held grimly to a door strut.

Moussa looked at him, the whites of his eyes large and frightened, 'This place is bad. Very bad!'

It happened in that split second of turning his head. A sharp jagged rock caught the edge of the left front tyre and in an instant it was flat. Before Moussa could bring the vehicle to a stop it slewed and hit another rock. His foot jolted off the accelerator and the car stalled, lurched to stand-still.

'Oh, Boss.'

David leaned over, across his driver, and switched the ignition off; got out to look. They had two deflated and split tyres but seemingly no other damage. More importantly the radiator was intact as were the gearbox sumps.

'Come on Moussa, let's fix this lot.'

But Moussa remained where he was: fixed, frozen in his seat.

Alone, David unloaded spare wheels and a large hydraulic pump jack. He dragged a squarish shaped boulder closer.

'Moussa, you'll have to get out, even if you don't help me.' David's exasperation was coming to the surface.

There was a slight delay; then the driver's door opened and Moussa was next to him.

'Sorry Boss, sorry for accident.'

'That's ok. We'll jack this side up and wedge that boulder under the front suspension. Then we'll jack the other side up and change that wheel first. When that wheel is on we'll jack this side up again and remove the boulder. Should be able to get the other one on then.'

Even so, it was physically laborious time-consuming work. In order to prop the vehicle up they had to scramble underneath it and clear the loose debris away. Moving a flat stone into place, Moussa disturbed an angry scorpion, a deathstalker, its tail coiled to strike. He jerked back and hit his head on the bumper; sand and congealed blood now covered his face.

Eventually both replacements were done.

David looked at his watch, said nothing. It had taken more than four hours. He lifted the second damaged wheel up to Moussa who was standing on the roof-rack when a shadow caught the periphery of his eye sight.

Then another and another .... and another ..... and another ....

Chapter 12
Contemplation

'He has only been gone for a few days and I miss him so much,' she mused. 'This new life for me, these past nine months together. This man who has changed my world. My David.'

Tecwwa looked around. The changes still surprised her.

A proper bathroom had been built complete with an overhead reservoir tank feeding water to a shower and flush toilet. A small solar installation gave enough power for lighting and a little refrigerator. Another room had been added, her treatment room, with neat cupboards and shelves to store medicines and raw materials. There was a low reed bed covered with a brightly-coloured straw sleep mat. A pretty pink and blue batik wall-hanging decorated one wall.

To one side of her home a small vegetable garden had been established; the plants green and tidy, so in contrast to the harsh surroundings. A few carefully protected saplings planted. The palisade fencing around the animal enclosure had been strengthened. In the centre of one panel hung a swing gate fitted with a locking bolt. And down in the village the local men had started to build the single class-room school she and David had promised the community.

In her mind she tried to estimate where he was, tried to recall the route from the map he had shown her before leaving.

'One day to Douentza, another day to Gao, then to Kidal. They must be nearly there. Ready to start out.'

Tecwwa sighed.

'I should have gone with him, but now it's too late. He understands why I was so apprehensive.'

She gazed out towards the north east. It was late afternoon and the far horizon was already cobalt-dark.

Opening her leather-bound jewellery box she lifted out the beautiful bracelet David had given her. The colours so in symmetry, glowing in the last sunlight. Admiring the bracelet as she always did, Tecwwa touched it to her lips.

'For twenty years, more than half my life I live with no-one. I have no-one. I need no-one. Now three days pass and I cannot bear to live without him.'

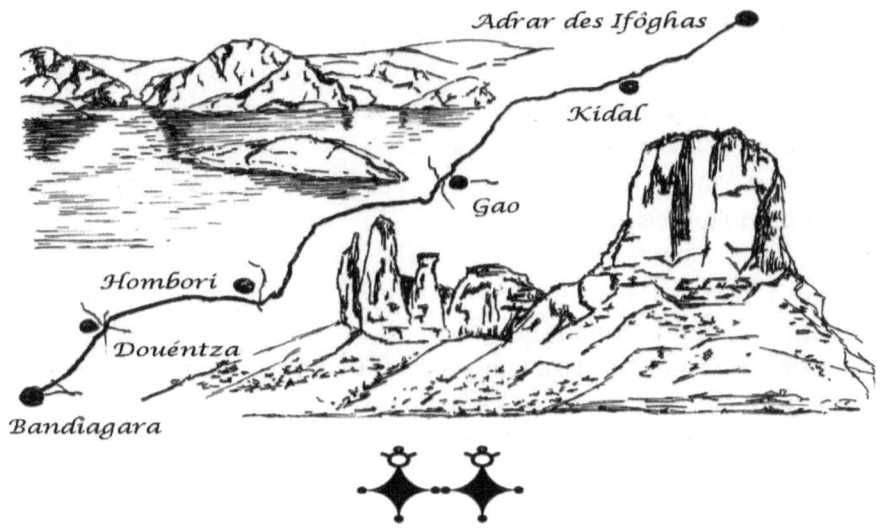

Chapter 13
Maimed

 Ten heavily armed men surrounded them.

It was apparent that they had been waiting for the Land Rover to be repaired before making their presence known.

With his revolver pointing directly at David, the leader gestured that they move away from the vehicle.

Not a word was said as two of the others searched the vehicle, quickly determining that David and Moussa were unarmed.

Time and sound appeared stopped, stilled, as captors and captured studied each other.

The leader stepped nearer. Like his men, he was dressed in plain khaki combat clothing. They all had off-white turbans on their heads and around their faces.

He looked at Moussa and said a few words. The language was guttural and impossible to understand.

'What is he saying?' David asked.

Shrugging his shoulders, 'it is not a language I know,' Moussa waveringly replied.

The leader beckoned another of his men over, said something to him. There was a pause before the second man spoke, then. 'If you try to run we kill you.'

'What is this one saying?' David repeated.

'It is Fulani language. If we run we die.'

'What do they want from us?'

Moussa spoke to the man, who turned and translated to his leader. There was an exchange of words, instructions, before the translator spoke again.

'You must not resist. You must go with us. Now!'

David stood his ground. 'Tell them we will not. We are touring. We are now going to drive on. Tell them.'

He could see that Moussa was shaking, filled with fear.

'Boss, I cannot, they will kill us.'

'Tell them.'

Visibly unnerved, Moussa followed David's instructions. His words caused the leader to come over to David. David stood firm, looked the man squarely in the eye, saw the fury lying there.

With a noisy glottal hawk he spat into David's face, a thick glob of yellowish nicotine stained phlegm. He spat again.

Before David could clean his face, the leader pointed his revolver and fired. As David collapsed in agony he could see where the man had shot him. The front of his walking boot was destroyed, blood soaking his sock where the toe had been blown away.

There was another sickening blow; the revolver butt slammed into the side of his head, a white-lightning scorch passed behind his eyes. He fell down, unconscious.

Chapter 14
Falcon returns

Tecwwa gazed eastwards, her mind troubled.

It was the time of the harmattan; the hot wind which sweeps off the Sahara. A wind that pushed sand and dust over vast areas. This was when the local people become irritable and uneasy. Even the domestic animals turn restless.

And her thoughts were like that wind; swirling, hazy and unpredictable.

A fear lurked within her. She knew something was very wrong.

There had been a wrench; a force which had startled her during the previous night. At first she wondered whether the wind had damaged her house or blown a section of the palisade down.

Lying on her mattress in the dark, she realised that the wrench was within her. It appeared to be like a disturbing dream which she could not properly remember. For the rest of the night she stayed awake; worried and confused.

Now, looking towards the horizon, Tecwwa listened to the sounds of the village awakening; animals herded out into the countryside, babies crying as they were being washed; wood chopped for cooking fires. The lowing of the cattle.

She also heard something more. A harsh "*kak-kak-kak*" sound modulating into a high pitched whine.

Focusing her eyesight towards the russet escarpment, she caught brief glimpses as the bird glided in and out of view; around and then behind the high rocky outcrops.

The memory of the first time she and David bathed together in the pure mountain water flashed through her mind. And followed that night when they made love for the first time. David physically so gentle and careful. How wonderful it had been.

But now the falcon was back. The big bird that brought tidings!

Tecwwa stood there for a long time, trying to envisage the message. What was the bird there for? And why at this time of the year?

A shudder went through her.

'Something has happened. My David, where are you?'

Chapter 15
Gallery

Extravagant whirls of colour, white and black and ochre and yellow and red; beautiful little figurines, delicately shaped roundheads; finely drawn wild animals, lions, ostriches, antelopes and giraffe.

He lay there in stupor, shocked and icy-cold. Slowly his blurred eyes took in the surroundings as his body adjusted hesitantly back into consciousness.

Turning onto his side, David looked around. They were under a huge overhanging rock, a vast open-sided sheltering cave. Sitting looking out across the valley, were two of his captors. At the far end of the shelter was a large fireplace, cooking pots and other utensils scattered around it. To one side sleeping mats were rolled neatly and heaped up.

This must be some sort of hide-out, he thought groggily. *I wonder where Moussa is?*

A blanket lay across his legs, he pulled it up and slowly started to feel warmer, drowsy, fell asleep again.

The pain woke him up. Not only was it the hammer-pounding in his head, but the raw pulsating hurt where he had been maimed.

Groaning, he twisted into a sitting position.

'Boss, have some water.'

Hazily, his eyesight still out of focus, David could see that Moussa's wrists were bound together in front of him, a tin mug clenched in his palms.

He took the mug and drank deeply. It was the sweetest liquid he had ever tasted.

'My foot, we need to clean it.'

'It's okay, Boss. They made me bring the first aid kit and other things from the car. We have cleaned and burnt it.'

'My God, burnt it?'

'Yes, when you were knocked out. One man took iron rod from fire. Afterwards I put plenty antiseptic powder and bandage. We will clean again tomorrow.'

'My toes?'

'One toe is gone. Second small one.'

David lay back, thoughts in maelstrom. Slowly and deliberately he pulled himself together.

'Where are we? What is happening?'

'Boss, I'm not sure. The one that speaks Fulani says they are waiting for other people to tell them what to do.'

'Other people?'

'Yes, Boss. I don't know who.'

'Where do these men come from?'

'These are Toubou. From Tibesti.'

'From Tibesti! That's more than a thousand kilometres away!'

'Maybe further, Boss. Nearly sixteen hundred.'

For a moment David was nonplussed, his mind working with information. The bandits came from Chad! Whatever were they doing here?

When the bandage was removed the next morning, he was surprised to see how effectively the wound had been cauterized. Scabbing had already started and there appeared to be little infection.

One of the captors brought boiling water over. David cleaned the mutilation painstakingly, treated and applied a fresh dressing, swallowed two Ibuprofen tablets.

Once again he was given water to drink, followed with a

couscous and vegetable broth to eat.

The foot hurt viciously, but at least the headache was diminishing and his vision had cleared; perception and thought processes gradually returning.

One thing was becoming clear.

They were being kept alive for a purpose.

Otherwise nothing made sense.

In this vast wilderness, he and Moussa could be disposed of so easily. One bullet each: their bodies left out anywhere. Hyenas and jackals would consume their remains with alacrity.

They must have a plan for us, he thought, *I wonder where Moussa is?*

Reclining on his sleeping mat he slowly closed his eyes. Suddenly something struck him.

With a start he opened them, looked wide-eyed upward.

His vision traversed from side to side, took in the sweeping scenes above him.

'Look at that,' he whispered to himself in awe.

He blinked again, as if to ascertain that what he saw was real. It was more than real.

It was genuine and wonderful. A gallery of masterpieces, some linked and some stand-alone, covered the surfaces of the overhang.

David searched through the few possessions that had been left next to him. The torch had been taken, but a small pen-light remained in a pocket of his jacket.

'This is just stunning!' he exclaimed aloud, pointing the tenuous beam. One of the guards pivoted to look at him quizzically, but after a moment turned away again.

A vast rock art gallery, the like of which he had never seen before, and, as his gaze took it all in, the like of which he was certain had never been found or recorded before.

Scenes of antelope prancing, delicate legs and horns finely depicted. Scimitar horned oryx in large herds. There were lines of elephant filing in and out of view, painted in a beautiful blend of brown and white. Tall outlines of yellow ochre giraffes, their coats accurately blazoned with black markings.

On the more rounded surfaces, hippopotami had been drawn to blend in with the stratum. And near them, unusually, there were even birds, flocks of golden crowned cranes and white storks.

But there was much more.

In the poor light he could just make them out. Great round-headed archers and warriors. Hunting parties. Women with white bracelets and anklets who appeared to dance in the curvatures of the rock face. Diminutive gyrating children.

A few large god-like figures were drawn high up, seemingly to look down on those long-gone original cave dwellers and artists.

'This is a prehistoric temple,' David said to himself; 'this is a miracle, just incredible.'

He tried to stand to get a closer look, but the pain in his foot was too intense. Sinking down, on his knees he shuffled closer to the sides of the cave.

A guard shouted; something like, 'halt!' but after watching David cursorily, realised that there was no threat.

'These paintings must be fifteen thousand years old,' David muttered. 'There are even areas that seem to have two or three layers of artwork, one on top of the other.'

Chimerical shapes and illusory outlines filled another frieze. They banded around a huge medusa-like form; what seemed to be an amorphous hybrid of a jellyfish crossed with a beaked octopus. Brown hand-print profiles and weird circular blobs formed a wave to one side.

'Fertility sketches or is it something more ethereal?' he wondered.

On hands and knees he crept to another corner. Here the scenes were unusually vivid. Animals mating, an elephant mounting another, and, similarly, numerous pairs of lions. There were men-figures with erect phalluses, heavy breasted women on slender frames. And small lifelike illustrations of men and women making love, in matching poses to the animals.

Laboriously he returned to his mat. Lying there, his mind marvelled at the ancient gallery. 'There are no modern animals, horses, cattle or even camels,' he reflected, 'and there are probably artefacts and stone tools littered everywhere.'

But steadily the wonderment dissolved as the situation facing them returned.

How the hell are we going to get out of this predicament? If only Moussa had been more careful. Quickly he dismissed the censure; they were in too much trouble to apportion blame.

Where is he anyway?

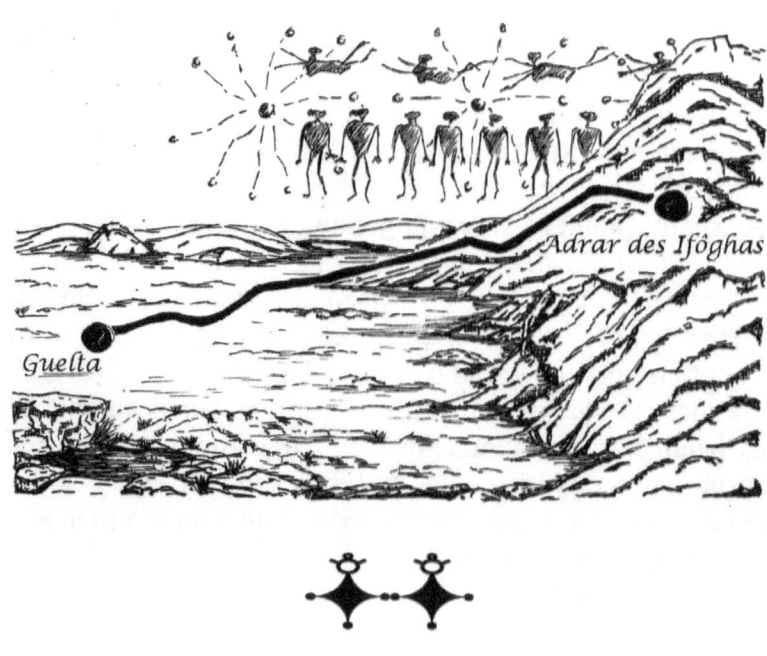

Chapter 16
Assiwi

Even though she was distracted by her worry for David, Tecwwa knew that her work as a medicine woman had to continue.

Everyday she was called upon to apply her remedies.

With careful kneading movements she palpated the Bella woman's stomach. Under her touch, the area felt hard-knotted and cramped.

Walking over to her table to prepare the medication, she left her assistant Tana to hold the woman, almost in a close cuddle. Her room, the one in which she treated and consulted, was a refuge where public reserve and restraint did not apply.

In this the dry season, food was scarce. She knew that the Bella had probably not been eating properly, if at all; living off scraps, wild fruit and tubers, giving whatever she found to her husband and children first.

Now she had come to Tecwwa for help.

Tecwwa mixed the ointment she wanted to use; a blend of ash, camphor and melted butterfat. From a jar on her shelf she removed a small piece of *pied d'eléphant* tree root. Cutting a sliver she then immersed it in a thin infusion of *assiwi* which was coming to the boil over the fire.

When it was ready Tecwwa returned to the woman in Tana's arms and spoke quietly. 'Please drink this, just sip very slowly.'

The Bella grimaced at the taste.

'Just slowly,' Tecwwa instructed.

When the cup was empty, they helped the ill woman to lie down; made her comfortable and relaxed.

Tana talked soothingly while Tecwwa applied her therapy, spreading the emollient substance she had made onto the woman's stomach.

Gently firm she massaged the area, first in complex circular movements followed by long smoothing strokes. Her knowledge told her that severe constipation was the problem; within twenty-four hours, the Bella woman would start to feel better.

From a bucket Tecwwa ladled *eghale* into a small milk can, wrapped some fresh bread into a cloth.

'Tomorrow when you feel better, you eat a little with this *eghale*,' she said.

'What is it?'

'This *eghale* is very good, very nutritious. Dates and millet and goat cheese. But only for you, to help you get strong again.'

The Bella nodded her head in gratitude.

For once the small chit-chat and reassuring attention integral to her caring, she left to Tana.

Tecwwa sat with them for a while, oblivious to their quiet talk; lost in her own thoughts, lost in her worry for David.

Chapter 17
Salesman

And where was Moussa? It had been close on four days since last he had seen him.

David stared up into the dark, sleep eluding him. So many thoughts were going through his head.

Probably it was the incongruousness of it all.

He, a white South African, lying incarcerated in a vast cave in Mali. He presumed they were still in Mali. A cave which bore ancient, mysterious artwork. An undiscovered place, undisturbed for thousands of years. A place of worship to life and internal spirit; to the surroundings and natural environment of centuries past. A place not dominated by an unseen and uncaring all-powerful god. What messages would archaeologists and experts find here?

He, a white South African, held captive by infiltrators from Chad. What were the odds on that! Why had he and Moussa been captured in the first place? And now being kept alive? Of what value were they and to whom? The circumstances that had led to where he found himself now. And how were he and Moussa going to conjure an escape? He didn't even know where Moussa was, let alone find a way to be released.

He, a white South African, loved, and was loved by a Tuareg woman. A perceived crossing of the racial barrier; something so unfairly illegal in the apartheid-dominated days of his youth. The way in which his life had changed since meeting Tecwwa. The wonder of it, and now the worry. If she knew of his plight; what would she be going through?

Everything seemed surreal, as if from some parallel world, so out of place.

David knew that he had to keep his mind strong.

In the daytime it was easier. His foot was healing and he was able to stand and hobble around slowly. Hours were spent sketching the rock art surrounding him.

He was no artist but owing to his engineering background, had become a competent draughtsman. His little notebook was rapidly filling with neat and accurate sketches.

More than once David found himself saying, 'I need to do this in order to prove to the authorities that this place really exists. This site needs to be preserved.'

The Chadian sentries watched with quiet amusement, making no attempt to stop him.

And David observed them too. Four men guarded him, two through the day and two at night.

I wonder where the rest of them are? And Moussa, too?

But at night it was difficult to sleep. Memories of Tecwwa and the times they had shared gave him positive strength, mentally sustained him the most...

They were on their way by bus. Whitey and Marie were waiting for them in Ouagadougou, both keen to meet Tecwwa for the first time. From there they all planned to visit Benin. Moussa had stayed behind in Ouahigouya to have a repair done on the Landrover. He would catch up with them later.

There was a line of orange traffic beacons crossing the tarmac road and a luminescent triangle propped up by a large rock.

As the decrepit bus lurched to a halt, a well-dressed man stepped out from under a shady tree at the roadside. A discussion followed with the driver and a banknote changed hands. Within minutes they were on their way again. The beacons, triangle and a large cardboard box carefully stowed next to the driver's seat.

From the box the man took out two large packets of sweets and a wad of pamphlets which he distributed personally to everyone on the crowded bus. Even to Tecwwa and David.

Nobody seemed to mind the two of them, even though they appeared to be so out of place. It was as if a white man travelling with a robed Tuareg woman, her head scarf covering much of her face, was just a normal everyday occurrence.

Everyone was more interested in the man and his sweets.

From the front of the bus he stood up and began speaking. All the Burkinabè passengers gave him their polite attention. Even the driver half-listened, half-watched, too.

He took two bottles from his jacket pockets, one large and one small, held them both high in the air.

In a language mixture of Mossi, French and Lobi, he described the contents of the bottles. David didn't understand a word and tried to read the pamphlet.

'What is he saying?' he whispered to Tecwwa.

'He is salesman,' she whispered from behind her scarf. 'He is selling tonic.'

On the pamphlet the only words David recognised were ginseng, aloe, menthe, castor oil: the rest were unintelligible.

In a hushed voice, Tecwwa said, 'I don't think we need to buy.'

An inflection in her voice made David scrutinise her closely. In her eyes he detected something, but then she turned away to watch the salesman at his work.

He was very good. For just the right length of time he extolled the virtue of his product, his voice charming, face beaming and smiling, gesticulating, rubbing his stomach, a few small suggestive hip movements. Slowly moving down the aisle with his box he took orders and money. Business was brisk. Bottles changed hands. More sweets were dished out.

The bus stopped and with a cheerful wave the salesman was off. As they started up again, David looked back. There he was, setting up his roadblock again, waiting for a bus travelling in the opposite direction.

99

After a while David felt Tecwwa shaking next to him. He leaned towards her, concerned. This was, after all a major journey for her. The first time she had been away from her home in twenty years, amongst different people, far from her normal environment, travelling with him.

He worried about the stress she may have been feeling. 'Is there something wrong? Do you want me to ask the bus driver to stop?'

'No, no.' But the shaking, if anything, increased.

'Tecwwa, please let me help you.'

With a small gesture, she lowered her head scarf, bared her face completely. It was then that David realised that his beloved, his normally reserved Tuareg lady, was not agitated or suffering from fear or anxiety at all. Tecwwa was giggling; half suppressed uncontrollable giggling.

'We do not need to buy,' she spluttered.

His obvious bemusement didn't seem to help. If anything it made her laugh even more. Eventually her self possession returned.

'What was that all about?' David enquired with a smile.

'Sexual anaemia.'

'What?'

The laughter surfaced again in her voice. 'That salesman, he says his tonic is good for all illness. For constipation, for lack of appetite and ... that is why we do not need to buy.'

She could hardly contain herself. 'For sexual anaemia.'

David had promised Tecwwa that they would take a holiday, go to Pendjari and see the wild animals. Animals that she had only heard about and never seen: lion, giraffe, elephants, baboons, waterbuck and roan antelope.

The meeting with Whitey and Marie was so relaxed. Tecwwa was absorbed into their friendship with an easy grace and gentle protection.

But before they had even left Ouaga, Marie whisked her away

to the more upmarket shops.

'Just give me your wallets,' Marie said to David and Whitey, 'we have things to buy.'

That evening in the privacy of their hotel room David saw what had been purchased; new clothes and underwear, two pairs of sandals.

'Are you comfortable wearing these?' he asked. The jeans and matching tops displayed her fine tight figure. And her new underclothing, when compared to her old worn out grey ones, were skimpy and sensual.

'My David, I am two women now. One who lives in the desert, who fell in love with a Western man. And also one who must be like a Western woman who loves, very much loves, the same Western man when in his world.' Her words and face were serious; but her eyes shone with happiness.

From Ouaga the couples made their way into Benin.

The first evening on the road they stayed with a local family who had turned their compound into a small auberge. They invited them to a local celebration party.

Their host explained the ceremony. 'This is a death party. We also have party for marriage or when woman becomes pregnant or when baby is born.'

'Who died?' Whitey asked.

'Village elder, important man.'

All the villagers were assembled. The men gathered together in pre-determined groups, all carrying a weapon of sorts, home-made spears, old muskets or sabres, shotguns, batons. All of them wore something on their heads, even if it was just a feather.

They strode and strutted, danced and chanted, marching in organised bands; up and down the street in front of the deceased man's house. Some were not so orderly. There were those that mimicked drunken soldiers, purposely marching out of step, some turned left, some turned right; somehow they managed to avoid collision.

There were men absurdly dressed, clothed to look like clownish animals wearing skulls or horns of animals long wiped out. Then there were the "brave" ones, throwing live chickens with their legs tied to sturdy sticks, down on the ground in front of them. Every so often the poor fowls were picked up and flung again.

Marie took a deep gasp, 'I can't watch this.'

Tecwwa took her arm and said quietly, 'We all have strange customs, even I not like, but we must tolerate.' There was a close moment as Marie appreciated her new Tuareg friend.

Dressed in their finest, the local women and children were voluble and excited. They were not supposed to dance, but slowly got drawn in. They lined up behind the "brave" men teasing them on. Others draped scarves around the more senior older men, a sign of respect and veneration. Many of the ladies carried bowls filled with food, fruit and drinks, which they distributed to the dead man's family.

Up and down the cortège continued.

An enormous python skin was hauled out, carried on the heads of some of the marchers.

At times the marching appeared intimidating, but it wasn't. It was just a wild, sometimes slightly inebriated celebration of the late man's life.

All the dead man's cattle were herded together in the village square, representing his wealth and esteem in the community. A terrified calf was dragged and tugged into the procession, the sacrifice that would feed the parading men later.

After about two hours, towards the end, the deceased's wives and some of the village elders moved around the gathering, touching hands with those they knew, thanking others for attending.

The visitors were thanked too.

'Can we give them a gift, some money?' David asked the host.

'No, no,' the man replied, 'tomorrow we will visit them in their huts. This is more important, more respectful. They are already talking about your group. About meeting your women. Where you come from.'

And four days later when they passed back through the village *on the return journey there was the sight of thirty or more old women sitting outside the dead man's house. They were keening and wailing; the sound ebbing and flowing.*

Mourning will go on, they were told, 'until the moon circle is full again.'

'Jislaaik,' *Whitey murmured admiringly, 'your Tecwwa is easily the most beautiful woman I have ever seen.* Prydferth iawn.'

They had stopped to camp along the Bori river. Trickling steadily down from the plateau a series of small rapids tapered down into a deep pool. Earlier a few young girls had been down with their water pails, but now it was just the four of them. Small birds flitted in the riverine undergrowth, a proud little malachite kingfisher perched on an overhanging branch.

How Marie had persuaded Tecwwa to wear a bathing costume, David did not know. But she had. And that the two of them had formed a bond was beyond question. David thought Tecwwa saw in Marie a way to learn western ways; absorb the good, sift out the bad. And Marie was enjoying the adventure, enjoying her role of female mentor and confidante.

The miniscule bikini the French woman wore did little to hide her very white and slightly opulent body. Tecwwa on the other hand, in her high-cut one-piece swimsuit which accentuated her shapely buttocks, looked exotic, looked almost out of place. Her wonderful body, her black hair gleaming in the dappled sunlight, her golden skin; she appeared demure yet captivatingly sexual, mature, and yet in so many ways still a young woman.

And as Whitey had remarked so candidly, she was the most beautiful woman David had ever seen, too.

On the very sultry evenings Tecwwa and David always made

their bed outside, up on the roof of the house. They lay there, whispering for hours, until the temperature cooled a little and sleep was possible.

There seemed to be so many things to talk about, so different their lives had been. And after their holiday spent with Whitey and Marie, Tecwwa now had a better understanding of where David came from. The reserve she displayed in public completely dissolved when they were alone together.

Tecwwa talked more of her mother now.

'As a girl I learn from her only medicine and touch knowledge.'

Tecwwa explained how she was taught to search for plants and herbs locally. How others were brought from traders and nomads. David had observed her doing it, even climbing trees in order to pluck leaves and flowers.

'The treating of the spirit, of mind I not know. I too young to learn. Only senior women who practice medicine for long, long time can do this. Some of these women, their doors are closed.'

'Their doors are closed?' David asked.

'They study Koran and Arab Text, even other Books. They have become pure, have become ... there is one word for it, but I not know.'

'I think you mean celibate.'

'Celibate, this means no more to make love, no sex?'

'Yes,' he answered.

She nodded in agreement, 'that is right word.'

Every so often they sprinkled water onto the mattress so that it was cool to the touch of their naked bodies. And their caresses on each other were languid and indulgent.

'You know why we like to drink three cups of tea at night,' she said.

'No...o.'

'My people believe it is like this.'

Tecwwa fondled David's scrotum amorously.

'Believe it like what?'

'You must be patient.'

In the star-glow he could see her grin.

She kept stroking him. Enhanced by a silver necklace, he

found her nudity in that light highly erotic. She knew it too.

'We believe that the first cup is strong, too strong. It represents death, so we drink it quickly to get to the next.'

David alternately kissed her breasts, gently sucking the nipples until they were firmly enlarged.

'And?'

'The second cup we drink not so quickly. For this cup is medium strong. This represents life.'

Their arousal was quickening; her stimulation had made him fully erect. He could feel her stomach muscles rippling in excitement as his fingers slid down into her pubic cleft.

'We always drink the third cup slowly. This one is just right.'

'This one is like love.'

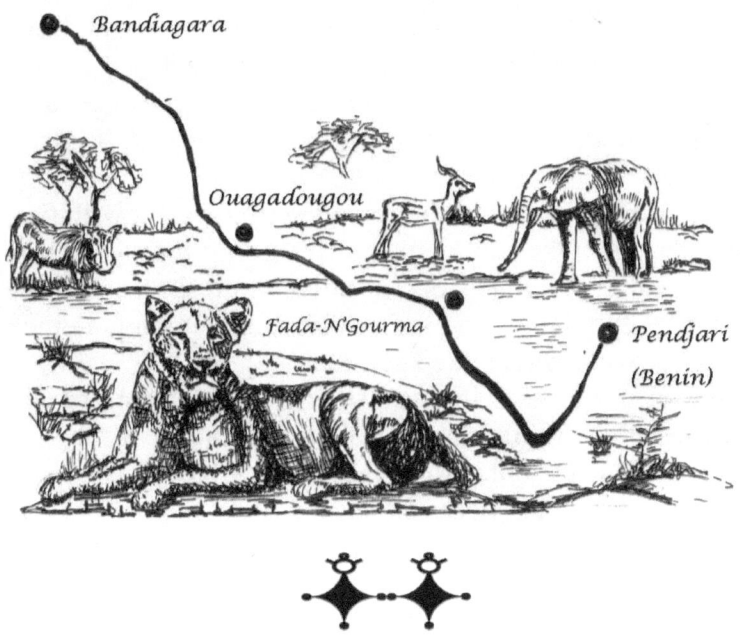

Chapter 18
Frankincense

The pure fragrance of the frankincense faded as Tecwwa sat there in the dark, unable to sleep.

It was like this most nights now; sleep for an hour or two, then awake, anxious and concerned.

The days just go past, she thought to herself.

David and Moussa left just when the wind started, now harmattan is almost finished. Nearly three months gone and no word.

Normally so frugal with her resources, and even with firewood scarce, she had taken to keep the fire going through the nights. From her small precious stock of olibanum resin tears, she would drop one in, the flames and the sweet subtle lemon pine incense a reminder of what David liked so much.

Tecwwa would gaze into the fire for hours, trying to visualise his face, believing the blaze to be a beacon for his return. David's unclouded blue eyes, the considerate all-encompassing smile that had brought her such peace. If only she could will him back.

David said they would be away for four weeks, but this is too long.

Sometimes the doubts would creep in. Had he left her never to return? Were their cultures too far apart for him to cope? Was the racial divide too deep? Had Moussa somehow persuaded him to leave? Never to return.

A depression would start to sink in. *My head will go into the wild.*

Quickly she would admonish herself. *What am I thinking? I*

cannot allow this to happen to me. It is not true. This is my David. I know him. He is an honest and honourable man. He loves me. And I love him, so much.

And still remorse would take over.

David had suggested that she go with them; go with him to find her family. He gently tried to persuade her but she did not want to leave.

'Why?' he asked.

'My David, it has been many, many years. I am so scared, afraid they all dead.'

'But don't you want to know, one way or the other?'

'My David, they left me here. They no come back. Maybe there is something they do not want me to know. Maybe they do not like me anymore. Not need me for daughter anymore.'

He looked at her carefully and tenderly wiped the tears from the corners of her eyes; silently acknowledging her explanation and reticence.

Chapter 19
Sheikh

 The stare was empty. Vicious saurian eyes not blinking or moving. Snake eyes. Like a deadly black mamba about to strike. They watched David without concern, without emotion; if anything almost ferociously pitiless.

Three days earlier his captors had led the white man from the cave. Stumbling along weakly, his foot, though healing well, was still agonisingly sore. A patched repair had been done to his boot.

After being in the gloom of the cave for so many days, he had to adjust and narrow his eyesight to the glare. Holding up his curved hands as a sunshield, David tried to find his bearings.

He looked around, but nothing appeared familiar. The rock formations and surrounding landscape were clearly of the Adrar.

But there was no vehicle, no car track, no Moussa.

The bandit group had also changed. There were definitely fewer of them. The leader, the one who had shot him, was no longer there, some of his cohorts were gone too.

In the shade of a few large apple-ring acacias a group of camels stood tethered together. David could see that they were all huge males. He remembered Tecwwa once telling him that the male camels were usually killed young.

And her slightly saucy aside, 'the stud male always belongs to the senior woman in the family.'

The largest males were nurtured and grown for two reasons only. One or two bulls kept for breeding, the others, always the biggest, utilised for smuggling, trained to cross mountainous terrains, silently and especially at night. The lighter faster females were kept for riding and trading.

The remaining men loaded the camels with their few possessions. They led David to one of the animals.

In response to a tug and sharp command, the camel knelt down. Gestures were made; David was half pulled, half lifted onto its back.

Until he got used to it, the swaying rolling gait made him queasy at first, but after a while he settled.

It's just the smell, David thought. *Never known anything like it.*

Bull camels are singularly flatulent and foul.

Now they were on the move heading north-north west out in the open air, the spare camels tied in a line behind them. David tried to imprint on his mind as much as he could. Landmarks, wells, directions of the watercourses, any unusual features; anything that may be of use in time to come.

A meandering trail to the south east was crossed. He wondered who used it. Elephants? Fula nomads? Smugglers? Or all three? Once, in a small open area of semi-desert grassland surrounded by low rocky hills, they came across some livestock; a few unattended animals in the middle of nowhere.

And after two days and nights of steady travel, he began to feel better. The animal's motion seemed to tone his leg and stomach muscles. There were times in the most difficult terrain where he had to walk as well. All this was improving his strength, making him fitter again. He felt mentally healthier too. The lengthy inactive time spent in the cave had made him introspective and brooding.

One thing he was sure of, something had to be happening. Break and rest periods were short, taken mainly in the heat of the day. They travelled through the nights. There was a driven purposeful air about his captors.

There was a destination or deadline to be reached.

Steadily its gait accelerated, he could feel the animals' stride getting longer and quicker. Ahead, in the distance, a few small buildings appeared shimmering in a mirage-sea.

'Must be a small oasis or well. The camels can smell the water,' David said to himself, 'They've been three days without any.'

As they got closer he saw that it was a *guelta*, a rocky depression filled with water.

And then David realised how far north they had come.

'I think we must be close to Algeria. Or maybe a bit more west,' he whispered, 'this doesn't make sense.'

And what he had thought were buildings were in fact not; *two vehicles, one looks like mine!*

Between the vehicles a sunshade shelter had been erected. Under it sat two men observing the incoming group impassively. One of them was the combat-clad bandit leader from Chad. David did not recognise the other, a man dressed a long ivory coloured robe and wearing a red and white checked *keffiyeh*.

All the other men were lying under the vehicles trying to find some shade. Only one of them stirred. A figure emerged, dusted himself down and slowly came over to David.

Moussa looked haggard and unkempt.

'Hello, Boss,' he said dejectedly.

David could see the despondency in his friend's face. And there was more. Some fear-filled premonition. It lay in Moussa's eyes. 'You look tired, old friend,' he commented sympathetically.

'Oh, Boss, if I not make accident, this big trouble not be with us.'

'We can't change destiny Moussa. We have to find a way out of this mess. We have to escape.'

His driver just shook his head. 'These are wild men, Boss. There is no chance. They will kill us for sure. Human life has no value to them.'

'Where have you been?'

'They make me drive to fetch Sheikh.'

'Drive to where? And who is Sheikh?'

'We drive to inside Mauritania. Then come here.'

'Mauritania! Whatever for?'

Moussa's eyes were hollow, his voice scared. 'We bring guns for Toubou people from Chad.'

'What do they bring in return?'

'Money, Boss. Much money. All dollars.'

'Dollars!' David's mind reeled as he absorbed the implications.

Dollars coming from where? The notorious regime in Sudan? The pirates in Somalia? The Chinese? The weapons going back; to Darfur or further south? Was somebody, some foreign government secretly arming the southern Sudanese to fight back against Bashir's thugs? Or was there an American involvement? Some covert conspiracy. Oil exploitation driving unrest.

'Why meet here?'

'Easy for Sheikh to travel in Mauritania and Algeria. Here, deep in Sahara. Everybody know of him. In main Mali, not so easy.'

'Know what of him?'

'Boss, this is Sheikh Saffah. In Arabic language it means People Slaughterer. People Butcher. This is terrible man.'

'I am tired of this Senegalese mongrel.' The English was clipped, almost militarily aristocratic.

David looked around. The Arab man in the *keffiyeh* stood right behind them.

Beneath the headdress the man's face was contemptuously proud and arrogant, slightly angular with a large hooked nose. A neatly trimmed greying moustache and full beard surrounded a small, slightly fleshy, pursed mouth.

David had never seen eyes that were so mean, totally void, almost as if artificial.

'What do you want of us?' he asked.

There was no reply.

David could hear Moussa take a deep breath, as if he knew that his enquiry would result in some violent reprisal. As if he was only allowed to speak in response to a question.

In that undisturbed silent desert landscape the silence seemed to clamour.

The vulture-like visage grimaced with distaste. With a furious fast swinging arm he slapped David twice in the face, first forehand then backhand.

'You only speak when I tell, no, *allow* you to,' the Arab hissed.

David studied him carefully, his cheeks stinging; an anger within him to retaliate.

From his belt the man withdrew a huge curved *khanja* dagger, pressed it to David's waist. He could feel the point go through his shirt just piercing his skin. The Sheikh was testing David's fury, testing his resolve to keep control, maintain dignity; he forced himself to calm.

The deep testing of his spirit, his soul, began in that moment.

When the screaming began they freed David from the Land Rovers bumper where he had been tied up, brought him out to watch. Two men held him vicelike, each with a knife to his face.

The Sheikh's men were torturing a stripped man, a man tied spread-eagled and suspended from a tree. A man whose blood and excreta flowed freely, horribly staining the sand below him. Their Chadian counterparts sat in a semi-circle around them, drinking tea and watching with grim enjoyment. The terrible smell and frenzied flies ignored.

In a large bloodied bowl were pieces of human flesh, skin that had been flayed from arms and legs; what looked like a nose and ears.

The poor suffering man's buttocks were now being systematically peeled, hanging in strips down the back of his thighs. Every so often one of the Chadians would get up, take a small piece of burning coal from the tea-brazier, push it down the victim's throat, forcing him to swallow.

When the terrible crying turned to squealing, the Sheikh

moved forward. With a callous grasp he took the man's penis and testicles in his left hand. Then, with a scything swing of the *khanja* in his right hand, cut them off; dropped them into the bowl.

David did not know when his friend died, for Moussa was in a dead faint after this last barbarity. He did know that Moussa was cut down and left. Left to lie there. Maybe still just alive. Before being torn apart and removed by the scavengers in the area.

All night long David could hear them; jackals and hyenas squabbling, competing for the remains. Early the next morning vultures were there too.

Chapter 20
Rumours

Compassionate and solicitous, Tecwwa looked at the crying Fulani girl who lay curled and miserable on her treatment bed.

She knew that the Fulani was hardly a girl; two babies already were proof of that. But lying there, to Tecwwa, she seemed so childlike and innocent.

Crouching down, she took the Fulani girl's hand into her own, with her other she soothed the girl's forehead.

'Ssh, my child, I am like your mother, and your mother's sisters, and like your grandmother and her mother before her. You can talk to me. You can tell me.'

The girl unwound, uncurled, lay there as if catatonic, eyes desperate and staring.

'Talk to me, my child.'

As if she were another being, from another world, the Fulani wept, pitiful and lost. The words were repeated and almost incoherent. 'A second woman, a second woman.'

'What, my child?'

'Second woman.'

'Your husband has taken another wife?'

'Ye...yes,' the Fulani girl whimpered.

'That is their way, the way it has always been,' Tecwwa said compassionately.

She knew how it was with these women. Jealousy was soon overcome as the two wives, most times, became like sisters. Their burdens and roles became shared and supportive; back-breaking manual work, child-caring, farming, homemaking.

'But I am still young. My body is still strong. My burrow is still tight. Why can he not take another woman when I am old, when I can no longer have children?'

'I understand your pain. Sometimes a Fulani man is impulsive. They do, then they might think.' Gently Tecwwa continued to massage the girl's forehead and temples.

The medicine woman and her patient sat there together; the disconsolate girl sobbing and wretched. Tecwwa knew that the misery had to purge. There was no hurry.

A random thought came to her, *I haven't seen Tana this morning, I wonder where she is?*

But just as quickly her attention returned to her patient. Leaning over, Tecwwa drew a small phial from her shelf, sprinkled a few drops of mahogany *neem* into a tin mug half filled with water.

'Drink, my child.'

The concentrated palliative had an almost immediate calming effect.

'Remember, my child, whatever you feel must be buried. However bad you feel, must be buried. You must do your work, your important woman's work. Your family work. It will bring you comfort. It is what we are born for,' Tecwwa's voice was like her hands, reassuring and sincere.

For a while the Fulani lay there, then gave a few small shuddering sighs and composed herself.

'My husband .... he has the body of an *arawa* and the brain of a *pentat*.'

After the girl had left, Tecwwa stood and looked out towards the village. A dust-devil swirled; through the sand-haze she could see someone running up the track towards her.

There seemed to be a desperation, a frantic arms-flailing urgency about the person: movements too quick, almost discoordinated.

Tecwwa waited; wondering.

Tana's sweat-and-dust stained face was etched with concern and exertion.

'Tecwwa, Tecwwa' she cried, 'you must come. Come with me. Men have arrived in the village, they are here now. You must talk to these people. Come!'

'Slow down, my dear. Why must I go to them? Start from the beginning.'

Grabbing Tecwwa's arm, Tana took a deep breath, gasped out. 'Come. These are Fula-Peul from near Tombouctou. They have brought cattle to trade with our Fulani.'

'And?' Tecwwa studied her friend and helper's face, trying to read the message there, within the depths of her eyes.

Then she knew the message.

'They have knowledge of David and Moussa?' she asked urgently.

Tana was near to breaking down. 'No...o, my cousin who is with them says they have news only of a white man.'

'And?'

'It is not good news.'

A claustrophobia, a dimness closed over Tecwwa. Her heart started to pound and she felt faint, sank to her haunches. Strength and composure drained in an instant.

'Is he dead?' she whispered.

Tana could not answer; in truth she did not know. Instead she knelt down next to Tecwwa. 'Go with me, we will share the news together.'

Around a small fire, six men were sharing a jar of millet beer. Greetings were extended yet subdued as they slowly, almost reluctantly, widened their circle to allow the women to sit with them. Tecwwa's seniority and status was undisputed, but it was not usual for Tana, as a younger single woman, to be allowed to join in. Some prior agreement and acceptance between the men had obviously been reached.

Tana was eager to confront the visitors but Tecwwa cautiously took control. 'Wait for them to talk to us.'

A moment of pause before the eldest of the visitors spoke. 'I see you, my sisters.'

'We see you too, my brother.'

Respectfully, Tecwwa continued.

'Your wives are well?'

'They are well, my sister. My youngest wife is with child.'

'May the new child be strong and good.'

'Thank you.'

'May your children be able to provide well for you in years to come.'

'Thank you.'

'Your family is well?'

'My family is well. My father is old yet still strong. Still walks with the cattle.'

'Your cattle are well? We hear of good rains.'

'My cattle are thriving. There is much for them to eat.'

'You appear to be blessed at these times, my brother.'

'Yahii provides for us generously, my sister.'

Tecwwa opened the palms of her hands. 'You are all welcome in our community. You are far from home.'

'All this land is our home,' and he gestured expansively around him, 'but yes, we are far from where we usually live.' In his wizened kindly face the old nomad had a pair of friendly inquisitive eyes. 'You are Tuareg, yet speak our language fluently.'

'I have lived here many years.'

One of the local men nodded in agreement. 'She can speak many languages!'

Briefly it was quiet as the man lit his pipe. He spoke. 'My brothers here, here from Dogon Country, say you are white man's woman.'

Tecwwa hesitated, absorbed the nuance before replying. 'Yes, that is true.'

117

'They say too,' and he gave a little smile, 'that the white is a good man and that you are *dokotoro*.'

'No, I am not doctor. I am medicine woman.'

'Yes, they tell me you help the sick people.'

Tecwwa nodded her head. Then she looked at the old nomad squarely and came straight to the point. 'My white man left before the *harmattan*. He should have been back long ago. I am very worried.'

'Where did he go to?'

'To Gao, then Kidal, then Adrar des Ifôghas.'

'Ifôghas is a very dangerous place for white people.'

Holding onto her for solace, Tana turned to Tecwwa, wanted to intervene and say something, but was sharply overcome, started to cry.

From the other side of the group another of the visitors uttered explosively, 'Tuareg woman, black woman should not have white man!'

Tecwwa was equally vehement in response. 'Why not? You see colour. You see black and white. You see racism. I see none. My David may be a white man, yet he sees none!'

'Shh....calm down. We share refreshment. We are friends and neighbours.' The old nomad raised his arms in appeasement.

For a while there was silence; the only sounds were the men slurping from the jar as it was passed around.

'My companion Tana here thinks that you may have heard something. May have seen something.'

'There are both, my sister.'

Again Tecwwa felt that clutch at her heart, tension gripping her very breath. But now she had to face it, be strong in the knowledge of what she might hear. In the grip on her arm she could feel Tana's anxiety, too.

'Please tell us what you know.'

'We were making our way to this place, to Dogon Country, when we crossed the path of others who were going towards the north. They went past us with camels.'

'Where was this? Did you speak with them?' Tecwwa queried.

'It was far away, near Kidal.' With a small stick he drew a

map in the sand for them to see.

'And?'

'These men looked aggressive, had many guns. So we hid behind high boulders and watched them. We could see they were not from these parts. Not from Mali, not from Niger, not from Burkina.'

'How do you know they were foreigners? Where do you think they came from?'

'From their dress, from their guns, from their very big camels. The saddles too were different. From the way they ride. Also they are in haste.'

'Between us,' and he looked around at his companions for confirmation, 'we think they are may be from Chad. Or border people with Libya. But we cannot be sure.'

Perplexed, Tecwwa and Tana looked at each other.

Tearfully Tana asked the next question. 'What else did you see?'

'One man on camel does not know how to ride. We also think his hands tied with rope.'

'What else?'

'We sure he is white man, he sit on camel like white man. Not know how to balance properly.'

Tecwwa drew a deep breath. 'Could you see his face?'

'No, very difficult, too far away.'

The old nomad sucked on his pipe, re-lit it with an ember from the fire. For a moment he held back the narrative as if to maintain suspense, but immediately realised that the women's anxiety was too great. 'There is something more.'

'Please my brother, we do not want to rush you, but we are very worried.'

'You know there are Tuareg in Hombori?'

'Yes, I have heard of them but I never been to that place,' Tecwwa replied.

'They are very upset, very cross. One of their fathers, an old man who lives in Kidal has been arrested, taken to Tombouctou.'

'What does this mean?'

'Patience, my sisters, let me tell you everything.'

Both Tecwwa and Tana looked apologetic.

'Also, the Hombori *gendarme* and the police chief from Douentza have been called to Tombouctou. There is big meeting with government people from Bamako.'

The circle of people was still. A sudden coolness in the air prompted a man to add a log to the dying fire.

'The Hombori people are also saying that the Mali army have captured a camel caravan. Near the east border with Niger.'

'And?'

'The camels were carrying weapons and ammunition. And that the smugglers were from Chad.' The nomad paused before continuing. 'These are the same men we saw.'

The man who had been rude to Tecwwa nodded in agreement.

'You are sure. How can you be sure?' Tecwwa asked as she absorbed the information.

'Yes, we are certain. It is because of the camels.'

And then it struck her. 'What about the white man?'

'Has he been found?' Tana interjected quickly.

'No, there are only rumours.'

'What rumours?'

'The police know that he is with another group.'

'Which group is this?' Tecwwa questioned.

'The rumour only is that they are Maurs. They are holding him for ransom.'

Still the two women wanted to know more. 'Where are these Maurs? How much ransom? Do you have a name?'

The old man shrugged his shoulders. 'There is nothing else we can tell you. Everything we know, you now know.'

In a corner of the room high up on a shelf a candle burned, illuminating the photograph in her hand.

Late into the still night she sat, looking at it, reading the inscription, turning it over and over. There was no thought of sleep or even preparing for bed.

All she could think of was what the visiting herdsmen had told her. A white man was in captivity, hearsay said it was for ransom. Somewhere beyond Tombouctou. In the hands of people from Mauritania.

'Could it be David? Is so, where would he be now? What had happened to him to be seized? Why has Moussa not come forward? Has he abandoned David?'

Pensively she repeated the questions out loud.

And then further memories also intruded. Reports of tourists and aid workers who had been killed by bandits in the last few years. Other Europeans held hostage after attending desert festivals; their governments paying money over for their release.

I know so little of these things, Tecwwa pondered, *if it is my David which government will help him.*

She shuddered and then was weeping: deep torturous sobs that hurt the core of her body, deep into the centre of herself. *And who will help me? This man is to me everything. If I lose him, they can bury me up on the cliffs with the Dogon. My life will finish.*

Who...who...will help me?

Unsteadily she stood, wrapped a blanket around herself and went outside. A faint rubescent blue, it was early dawn, slowly getting lighter.

From high in the sky came a familiar sound.

'The falcon is here once again,' Tecwwa whimpered, 'it is back.' She looked but could not see it.

'What are you holding? What are you holding?' The tone accusing and stern. 'What are you holding?'

She turned around, but there was no-one.

'It is me speaking,' Tecwwa whispered, 'my head inside is speaking. What am I telling myself?'

Standing there, she heard the bird cry again.

'I am holding the photograph.' Whitey had taken it; a picture of David as he was making fire when they were on holiday in Benin. Her David smiling and relaxed. And on the back in his neat deliberate handwriting were Whitey's words;

I am my Brother's keeper.

Tecwwa studied it yet again. The image of the man that she loved above all else, looked back at her.

Then it came to her, the falcon had brought her a message.

She knew what to do.

'You want to walk back with us, my sister?' The old man from Tombouctou was incredulous.

'Yes, my brother, that is what I want to do.'

'We move quickly. Our women normally follow behind on the donkeys. More slowly. '

'I will move quickly with you, my brother.'

'Do you trust us?'

'Yes, I see you as my father, Baaba. I trust you and your men.'

'They are not my men, but you can trust them too. They are like me,' the man smiled, 'but we do not go all the way. Our big herds are near Haribomo. The last way, you will be on your own.'

Tecwwa looked him in the eye. 'There are two from here that will go with me. Tuareg men.'

'Why will they go with you?'

'My white man, my David, he helped them before when one of them had trouble. There is honour to be repaid.'

The old man sat back on his heels, eyes half closed as he considered the situation. 'Why don't you walk to Douentza and take a bush taxi north.'

Again she looked straight at him. 'These local Tuareg men are known to the *gendarme* in Douentza and in other villages. In surrounding area. They prefer to walk. Besides, we have no money for any transport. We only have our feet.'

'And you can rely on them?'

'Yes, Baaba, I have no choice,' Tecwwa replied simply. 'We are Tuareg. Our codes are very strict. It is, and has become even more so now, their duty to protect me. And if my David is the one being held for ransom, it is also their obligation to help me find him.'

'You think that three Tuareg desert dwellers can do what the Government and military cannot?' His face was sceptical.

'We have packed our few things. We are ready to go.' And then she answered his question. 'There is no more time for waiting. I will find him.'

Chapter 21
Lizard

 What at first seemed to be a useless and pointless brutality was now David realised, not so. The Sheikh was openly proving to him, and to his own followers and cohorts, that when a person was of no further use, or if there was disobedience or dissent, a life could be wiped out. As easily as dowsing a tiny flame.

Feelings and sentiment, compassion; there was no place for that in their world. And he, the Sheikh was in charge of their world.

To get to grip with the shock of Moussa's murder, David knew that he had to get his brain under control. There had to be a way. The certainty was that he had to stabilise his thoughts, find a way of coping. But this was not easy. If he thought of the future, of release, he could not see it. If he thought of the past, could the love that he and Tecwwa shared succour him? Keep belief of rescue burning? Give hope for the future?

Something lay hidden in his memory, something Whitey had once said, *What was it?*

David sat huddled there for hours, hands bound to the Land Rover bumper. Going through his head were so many things. The notion of trying to escape, imagining he and Moussa could have attempted something. Thinking that he could possibly get word out, via a nomad or someone else when passing through a settlement; maybe try and abscond during the night. He had even thought of stealing a camel.

But the Chadians had left with all their camels fully laden. Weapons and ammunition destined to fuel a conflict where it was almost certain that the innocent and peace-abiding, the poorest, were hurt the most.

The vehicles were immobilised every night; distributor caps removed and handed over to the Sheikh for safekeeping.

A guard was always watching him. He was securely tied up. They were in desert terrain familiar to his captors; somewhere he had never been before.

He was hungry and filthy dirty. And Moussa was dead.

Now the futility of his situation was so clear to him.

Other than his two sets of captors and poor Moussa, David had seen no-one else since leaving Kidal weeks back, before all this had happened. Even the few cattle and goats they had passed a few days earlier appeared to have been unaccompanied.

The hopelessness of his situation was sending him down. Down into a depression, a wretchedness David had never known before.

An echo went through his head. It was from their shared military days, so many years ago. The saying had come back, Whitey's strong compelling voice:

When you are alone for a long time, on reconnaissance, on your own, in the heat or in the cold, you must keep your mind still. You must be like a concealed lizard. You must keep your mind still in your head. You must have a lizard mind.

PART 3

RESCUE

Chapter 22
Cry for help

'Monsieur Whitey, *s'il vous plaît.*'

The accent was unknown to her. A man's voice she was certain that she had never heard before.

'Monsieur Whitey, Monsieur Whitey!' Came the second request, the voice loud and imperious.

'He's not here,' Marie le Roux answered in French, 'he's at work!'

Marie could hear her reply being repeated to someone else, a third party. She was puzzled; Whitey very seldom received telephone calls at home and then only when there was an emergency at the Mine. But it was mid-morning, he was there now, this had to be something else.

For a moment there was quiet at the other end of the line. She listened closely, sensed that it was necessary; to be relayed to Whitey when he came home later. Marie heard little rustling sounds, then, 'hold the phone this way up.'

As if from underwater, an eerie faint voice spoke. 'Marie, it is I.'

'Who is it?'

'Marie, it is I, Tecwwa.'

'Tecwwa? David's Tecwwa?'

'Yes. Please, Whitey to help.'

In those few words Marie could hear it in Tecwwa's voice; an acute desperation and anguish.

'Tecwwa, what is the matter? Why are you phoning us? Normally David....,' and suddenly she realised. 'Tecwwa, where is David?'

'David gone.'

Nothing could hide the distress in those two words; not the distance, not the poor reception, not the fact that it was the first time Tecwwa had ever used a telephone. She was sobbing and trying to talk at the same time, totally incoherent.

'Tecwwa, my dear, let me speak to the man. Please, my dear.'

In the background Marie could hear men's voices. She pulled a scrap of paper nearer, looked at her watch and wrote down the time, next to it the number on the handset display. Whitey was fastidious about detail.

'Hallo, hallo,' Marie shouted.

'Madame,' came the reply.

'Please try and tell me what the problem is.'

'Madame, I am the *Maire* in Tombouctou,' the man articulated importantly.

'Please, *Monsieur le Maire*, please tell me what is going on.'

'Madame, this woman is Tuareg lady. There are two other Tuareg men with her. They only want to speak to your husband.'

'Why?'

'I do not know. They will not tell me.'

'Why are you helping them then? With telephone?'

'Madame, a Mali mayor must help his people. But I am a Bambara man. The Tuareg always refuse to trust us.'

Maybe for a reason, Marie thought fleetingly to herself. She deliberated for a moment, knew what to say, knew instinctively what Whitey would want her to say.

'Please tell Tecwwa, the Tuareg lady; Whitey is on his way.'

Sometimes, reaching compromise with his wife was not an easy thing to achieve.

'No, you are not!'

'I am going with you.'

'Cariad, dwyt ti ddim!'

'Whitey, I am.'

Whitey had never seen his wife more resolute. This was not

foot-stamping and tantrums, but a resolve of unbreaking determination.

He tried to reason with her. 'My darling, these are dangerous places. Beyond Tombouctou and along the Mauritanian border. And Niger and the southern parts of Algeria too. These days probably some of the most dangerous places anywhere in the world.'

'I'm still going.'

His companion, a huge black man, looked on solemnly, trying with some difficulty to conceal the humour he found in the situation. Whitey was definitely losing the argument.

'Whitey, take Salim. He is the biggest strongest man I have ever seen. And I'll speak to the local police chief. Get permission for one of his men to go with you as well. He'll be allowed to carry a weapon. And he can stay to protect Marie in Tombouctou if you decide to go further east or north east.'

Roger MacArthur, the Mine manager, was understanding and helpful. He knew David well, was his successor after all. Whitey didn't have the heart to tell him of the preparations already made through the previous night; rifles and ammunition hidden in the cushioning of the back seat of the double cab, revolvers carefully wrapped and hidden under floorboards; tear gas and smoke grenades concealed within the door panels. The weapons all taken from the Mine's substantial arsenal.

On the roof-rack of the Toyota Double Cab, under the spare wheels, was a long shallow steel box filled with spare parts. A totally dissembled sub-machine gun was squirreled away between the components. An array of knives, bayonets and home-made garrottes camouflaged inside a steel jerry can.

And now with his manager's help, an unsuspecting *gendarme* to accompany them. This would now probably ensure only the most cursory inspections at customs and police posts.

As they drove, the four of them in that heavily loaded vehicle; Whitey could feel the adrenalin pumping; the anticipation and thrill of a dangerous mission pulsing through his body. Outwardly calm, his mind was alive. He was like a caged leopard set free, eager, straining to be on the hunt again.

What did her words mean?

'Please, Whitey to help. David gone.'

Chapter 23
Blindfold

 He remembered once reading of a settlement like this; a small village with sweet-water wells that a wealthy Swiss-American had futilely tried to turn into a desert paradise, a market garden to supply others. Give the local people some employment. A place for the few passing tourists to stop over. Banditry and kidnapping had put an end to that.

And the nearest town of any substance was nearly three hundred kilometres away. The only road, if it could be found, was at most times almost impassable, as regular sandstorms swept over and covered it. Competing with the swathes of Sahara sand, the sun burned with unsparing ferocity every day of the year.

David could still see vestiges of where gardens and orchards were once laid out and cultivated; where piping and water-furrows had led. Now everything was forlorn and long abandoned.

About five kilometres north of the village they abruptly turned left, heading directly west. Through the thick sand the vehicles churned, regularly getting stuck. Tyres were taken down to 8 bar for better traction, lengths of old conveyor belting used as mats in the softer sections. Everybody had to push the vehicles, even he was freed, his arms unbound, forced at gun point to help.

Progress was tough and slow.

David observed the men around him. One he now knew as Ahmed had clearly been designated to guard him. *There is something in him*, David thought, *a slightly more considerate side, as if he is ashamed that I am a prisoner. Seems to go against his principles. Or maybe it's just my imagination.*

The other three appeared to be as hard and cut-throat as their leader. Sheikh drove the lead vehicle. David's commandeered Land Rover was driven by the youngest of the bandits. His approach was to thrash the vehicle through the gears, driving without care or skill.

Slowly the sand hills and low dunes thinned out, opening to surround a long narrow hard plain.

'A salt pan. Carefully compacted and marked,' David said to himself. 'Looks like it's been turned into an airstrip!'

In the distance he could see a sand-blasted flagpole with a ragged windsock, next to it a line of oil drums.

A neat row of tents and screens had been erected in the lee of a large single dune. Nearby a few tamarisk trees gave some sparse shade.

'I wonder if this is the Sheikh's base camp?'

There was a shout from the vehicle ahead. They stopped. Without warning, David was thrust face-down into the loading box. A knee pressed into his back as two men held him prone. He could feel his shirt being torn. A strip of cloth passed over his eyes and he was tightly blindfolded.

Almost inaudibly Ahmed said something in Arabic. *'Ana Assif. En'ne A'ataher, sayeedi.'*

David thought it sounded like an apology.

The taking away of his vision impacted deep within him, draining his optimism for survival. Whilst he could see, he could observe, could get a sense of where they were and who his captors were, their habits and tasks.

But now everything blurred away. Nothing seemed important, whether they brought food and water, whether they untied his hands and feet and walked him into the desert for his ablutions. Whether it was night or day or even if it was hot or cold. Whilst he could sense other activity around him, it felt as if he was being driven into hibernation and dormancy. Alive, yet removed from life. Like a tethered, slowly dying dog.

From the shelter they had rigged as his prison, he could occasionally hear sounds, especially if the wind direction was right. He knew that one of the vehicles had departed.

There had to be a satellite telephone, for on two occasions he made out a few audible words from the Sheikh's one-sided conversations. For security reasons the telephone was probably not used that often. Silence and isolated seclusion to the Sheikh's nefarious missions was vital.

One night from nearby in the dunes, he clearly heard two men's muffled grunts in their act of sodomy or mutual masturbation.

And in the mornings there were always greetings between the Sheikh's brigands, '*Allahu akhbar, salaam alaikum.*'

David knew what the words meant. For him there was no peace, there was no God to save him.

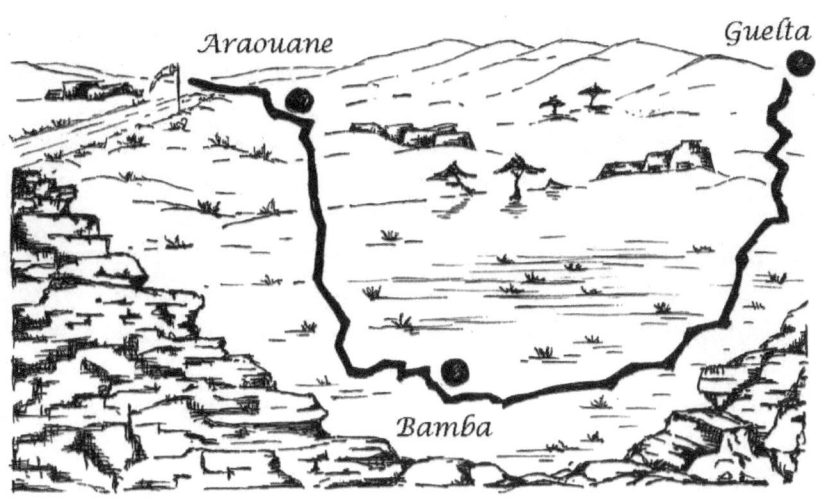

Chapter 24
Tombouctou

They had started out on the road well before dawn.

With eyes half closed, Marie watched her husband. She hadn't slept at all the previous night.

He would not let anyone else drive. From Segou to Niono, with its Great Mosque umber-elegant to their right. The road conditions steadily getting worse. Staying north of the Niger River, they passed Nampala, stopped to refuel in Niafounke.

Whitey's concentration was unwavering. Kilometre after kilometre passed by; so did the hours, sunrise to midday, midday to late afternoon.

In his heart, Whitey knew something was really wrong. For a woman as strong and resilient as Tecwwa to contact them was so unusual, so out of the ordinary, it had to be serious.

Repeatedly he made Marie go over her brief conversations with Tecwwa and the Tombouctou mayor. In between he spoke to Salim, getting the big man to make a list of things to find out or obtain.

The roadblocks came and went, most of the time they were just waved on, the accompanying *gendarme* assuring quick passage through them.

Marie could feel it too. Whitey's focused intensity was exciting. Their daily lives in an open cast mining environment were mostly humdrum and sedentary. Everything was always routinely monotonous.

Not now. Something had happened to their closest friend: what, where, when, they knew not. Yet within less than a day they were mobilised, on a crusade, however daunting or probably impossible, to find him.

She was afraid, and excited too…

'How will we ever find Tecwwa? This is quite a big place,' Marie asked, looking around as they drew near. Ahead lay Tombouctou, its overall shabbiness deflected by attractive skyline minarets. Partly disguised in the twilight, the town's outskirts sprawled untidily into the surrounding desert.

Whitey smiled, 'I am sure she will find us first.'

'How can you be certain?'

'At this time of the year we will probably be the only white people here. Word will quickly be on the streets. And Salim will definitely attract some attention.'

The giant, six foot six; one hundred and twenty kilograms of solid muscle honed by many years of traditional wrestling and weightlifting, just smiled.

His connection to David was equally valid. Through David he had obtained a referral which led to his job on the Mine. But there was more to it than that.

He was Moussa's eldest brother too.

'There is someone at the gate to see you, I am sorry to disturb your eating. I try to send them away, but they will not go.' The little restaurant owner looked unhappy. As if he could see valuable foreign currency evaporating with his news, precious clients being upset.

Whitey looked at Marie, raised his eyebrows. She just said, 'We have only been in Tombouctou for a couple of hours.'

'Wait for me here,' he instructed. 'Salim come.' To the *gendarme* at the next table, he pointed at Marie. The man indicated that he knew what to do, to watch over her in their absence.

Salim and Whitey stood at the entrance gate, carefully looking around. The street activity appeared normal, people going about their customary evening business. Across the road they could see three figures standing in the semi-darkness.

But still Whitey was cautious, his sharp eyes scrutinising the surroundings, all faculties alert. Something in Tombouctou did not feel right. He could sense suspicion and mistrust. Having only just arrived, he doubted whether anything was aimed directly at them. There seemed to be an underlying fear, he couldn't quite detect what it was.

But he would make sure to find out.

In this town, once the centre of enlightened Islamic scholars and study, where great trading parties had passed through; something just did not feel right.

'Stand still,' Whitey said, 'let's see what happens.'

Leaving the night-shadows one of the three moved; a person dressed all in black came towards them.

'I think it is a woman,' Salim whispered.

For a moment everything seemed static, frozen in time, then the approaching person swayed, folded, as if to fall.

In that instant, Whitey knew who it was. Springing forward he caught Tecwwa in his arms, lifted her up and carried her into the restaurant.

Over his shoulder he called to Salim, 'try and talk to the other two. Get them in here!'

'Thank you for coming to Tecwwa,' were her first words.

It didn't take long for Marie to mobilise the restaurant owner. A couch had been brought out for Tecwwa to lie on. Marie took over the kitchen, extra food was being prepared, chicken and nourishing millet in a crushed baobab leaf sauce; the owner's wife and helpers enjoying the bustle and activity. Tea had been made for Tecwwa's two Tuareg companions. Extra bread and hibiscus juice were already on the tables.

'We must find David,' were Tecwwa's next words. 'Please,

we must find him.'

'You will have to start from the beginning. We know nothing.' Whitey said calmly.

Even though it was clear that Tecwwa was exhausted and her clothes torn and dirty, in her eyes and in her voice there burned a resolve, a steadfastness of will.

Marie and Whitey could see this as they persuaded her to eat a little.

Taking their time they interrogated her gently. There were only two facts she really knew.

'David and Moussa left at the start of winds. They were going to Adrar to try and find my family.'

Whitey looked surprised. 'That's nearly four months ago.' He wondered why Tecwwa hadn't gone too, but held the question back.

'Yes, I wait and wait, very worried.'

'Why did you wait so long?'

Abashed, Tecwwa covered her face with her hands. Quickly Marie moved over and embraced her sympathetically.

'What could I do?' Tecwwa said bleakly, 'I have no money, no information.'

'Why did you not telephone?' Whitey asked.

She could not answer. Marie replied instead, 'Whitey, there are no telephones where she lives and she does not know how, has never learnt to use one.'

For a while nothing was said. From behind her hands, Tecwwa spoke. 'Even when I come here, I do not know, not sure, what to do. I know you work on big gold mine. David once tell me where. We go to local mayor. He get number, he phone to Marie.'

'What made you come to Tombouctou?'

Tecwwa's self assurance and composure slowly returned. She told of visiting nomads to the Dogon and the rumours they brought; stories of a white man being held by bandits, an old

Tuareg man from Kidal incarcerated, government and police meetings.

'You phoned us from the Mayor's office. Did you ask him? What was going on?'

'I try. But he just say, official matter, secret. Not for discussion with ignorant Tuareg woman from bush.'

Before Whitey continued with his questions, Marie poured out more of the hibiscus juice. The restaurant owner hovered around and she sent him off to fill the jug.

'So how did you get here?'

Tecwwa gestured to her two Tuareg escorts. 'We walk. With same Fulani nomads and the headman. He good man.'

'You walked? All the way from the Dogon?'

'Yes, we walk to Haribomo. Very quick. At night we sleep two, three hours. Then go on again.'

'And.'

'From Haribomo we are on our own. Headman stay there. We walk to here, to Tombouctou.'

Whitey took a map from his travelling pouch, studied it, calculated the distances.

'You walked two hundred and fifty kilometres in a week?' he said.

'No, less days, we sleep four times.'

Marie just shook her head in amazement.

'What happened next?'

'One of those men,' Tecwwa pointed to her companions, 'he has family here, one brother. We go to him. He say all Tuareg here talking about old man in jail. All Tuareg people here very cross.'

'Why?'

'They say the police, the Bambara men, beat him to get information.' She sighed. 'He old man, should be treated with respect.'

'What information does he have?'

For a moment she could not answer. Marie went over to Tecwwa again. She put her arm around her friend's shoulders.

'I not sure. There is report he saw two men in Kidal. Ask him how to get into Adrar, to the place where I was born.'

'So?'

'One man is white man. One man is black man. Car is Land Rover.'

Whitey nodded, 'and there is something more isn't there.'

'Again, I not sure. Only stories from Tuareg people here.'

'Stories?'

'There is English word. A word like rimes, rumes?'

'Rumours, maybe.'

'Yes, yes. Rumours. There is one rumour that bandits have white man as prisoner. And that white man and the white man seen in Kidal is same.' Tecwwa drew her breath. 'There is also second rumour.'

'And that is?'

'That the Land Rover seen in Kidal; it has been seen here too. In this town Tombouctou.'

'David!' Marie exclaimed.

'No. Nobody seen him. Land Rover driven by someone else. But people here not sure who.'

Tecwwa started to cry again, her shoulders shaking, head abjectly down. 'But my David must be near. I feel it. Inside me I feel it. But where he is, I do not know.' Marie hugged her tightly.

For the first time, Salim spoke. His voice was deep and stentorian from within his massive frame. 'And black man, driver of Land Rover?'

'Of Moussa. No news and nobody knows,' Tecwwa whispered.

It was late.

The restaurant owner came nearer, thinking they were finished, but the look on Salim's face frightened him away.

Whitey spoke firmly. 'We need to find out where David is. And Moussa too. Fast.'

'Tomorrow we start!'

Their little hotel room was basic and unpretentious. Yet it was clean. They had obtained a room for Tecwwa too. Marie had given her some toiletries and spare clothes.

With his thoughts prowling and widespread, Whitey observed two little night-lizards, geckos, stalking mosquitoes on the ceiling. He turned to look at his wife, could discern the ardent tension within her.

Marie was washing from a bucket of water. Somehow she managed to shampoo and rinse her hair; now soaping herself down, the soft desert water making the lather white and velvety.

The unknown risks ahead, the adventure, the planning, the danger; she knew Whitey was going to do something. He had said, 'Tomorrow we start.'

It made her so sexually intoxicated that when she washed between her legs, orgasm was almost on her.

Marie was aware that Whitey was looking. Arousal flushed her chest; one hand moving up to seductively clasp her breast, alternately caressing pink swollen nipples.

That night their lovemaking was intense and often and fast, without restraint or inhibition, the anticipated danger an enhanced stimulus for both of them. After all their years of precaution, of a reluctance to have children, this time there was none.

For during their passion, Marie and Whitey's first daughter was conceived.

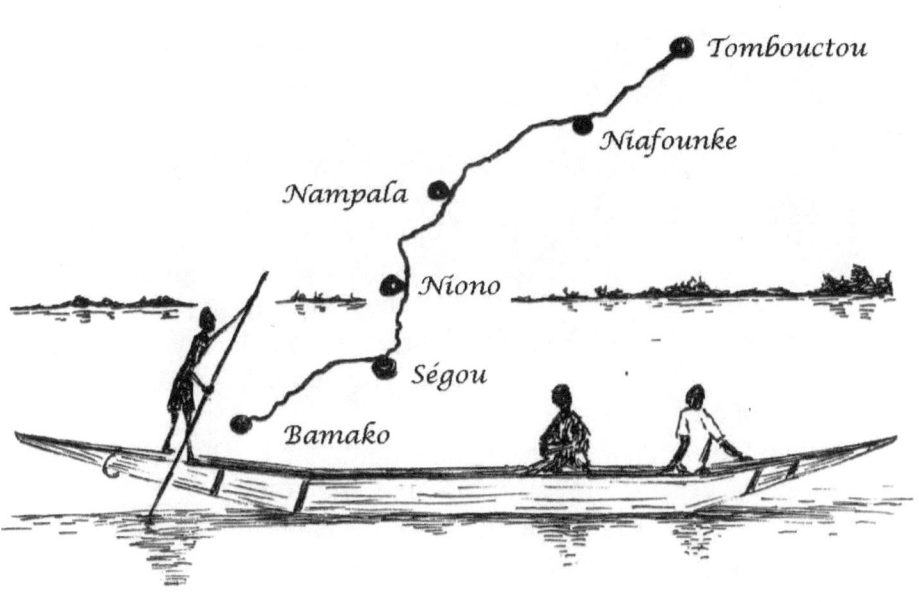

Tombouctou

Niafounke

Nampala

Niono

Ségou

Bamako

Chapter 25
Mission

'We are too conspicuous,' was the first thing Whitey said the next morning. At that early hour, there were only the four of them; he and Marie, Salim and Tecwwa. Marie had rustled the owner awake just after six am. The fact that they were up so promptly and in his restaurant had him scurrying around to provide coffee and breakfast.

Unveiled, Tecwwa looked fresh and rested. During the night she had succeeded in cleaning and mending her robe. The resolve and determination in her face and eyes seemed to be stronger than ever. Tecwwa knew that with Whitey present, a plan of action would unfold.

This man was like no other she had ever met. She had seen it when they had been together in Benin to see the wild animals. The time she and David had been together, in love and so happy. The fierceness and hardness, an iron control and discipline; a temperament very different to her David. But Tecwwa knew that there must be another side to him, a deep side that only Marie could understand and access.

From his pocket he drew out a piece of paper. 'I have listed the priorities which the four of us must do. Only we will know of them, they are not to be divulged to anyone else.'

'What about Tecwwa's companions and the *gendarme*?' Marie asked.

'As soon as I can I am going to put the soldier on the bus home. Pay his fare. Tell him we don't need him anymore as we're going no further. Give him a little extra cash for helping us so far. As for the other two we'll involve them as and when we need to, but not now.'

Both Salim and Tecwwa nodded in agreement.

'And Tecwwa, you and I are leaving Tombouctou when I know that the *gendarme* is on the bus.'

'What? I not leaving, Whitey!'

'Let him finish,' Marie said gently.

'Tecwwa, you must tell your friends there is nothing here for you, that I am taking you back home. By car. They can go with you if they want, but my guess is they'll stay here for a while. I'll give them some money too. For helping you. That should persuade them to spend it here.'

'I not go!'

Ignoring her, Whitey went on, 'What we are really going to do is to go back to Haribomo. It's only a few hours by car.'

'Why to Haribomo?'

'Somehow I don't think people in Tombouctou are going to help us. I want you to talk to the old nomad again. Ask him to move up this way with his cattle. Quickly. At the same time he must try and get information for us. I'll tell him what we want to know. If necessary I'll give him money too. We'll remain near him, in the desert, in the bush, wherever he is, until we know more.'

Tecwwa didn't hesitate. 'That is good plan. Old nomad will help. I sure. He ..... like me, impressed with me.'

'Good. Salim, you will remain in Tombouctou.'

The big man looked inquiringly.

'I want you to move around. In the bars, in the markets. You speak Bambara. Talk to local Bambara people. Not the government people. Tell them you are a wrestling champion and also a promoter, looking to bring a tournament here. Arrange some matches. Find a training partner. You know the Bambara enjoy wrestling. Get some children involved. Children always talk freely. So find out what they are saying. And what anyone else is talking about. But all without asking openly. I am sure somebody will know something.'

Whitey looked at his note.

'Also, we'll prepare a list of supplies you must get. Things we may need; like extra food and provisions. Buy in small quantities only, and regularly; as if you are looking after yourself on a day to day basis.'

Pleased at his role, Salim placed his hand on Whitey's arm. 'I understand.'

Marie raised her eyebrow quizzically.

Whitey grinned, a small mischievous cheeky twitch. 'You, my darling, are going to be the typical tourist. The solo Frenchwoman flirting with the local men, wearing traditional clothes, taking photographs of everything. Always on the go. Find out where bands are playing, go dancing. Have your hair done in African style, braids, or whatever they call it.'

'This is all too boring!' Marie exclaimed.

Gently teasing Tecwwa interjected, 'Let him finish.'

Salim's powerful voice also echoed humorously, 'Yes, Madame, let him finish.'

'But you will also do more,' Whitey went on, 'I want you to visit the libraries and museums. Pretend to look at everything. Also the old explorers houses, there are three or four of them with displays. Go there. Chat to the staff. Look at the maps particularly carefully. If possible take photographs.'

'Why? Will I be safe doing this?' Marie asked worriedly.

Whitey paused for a few seconds then continued. 'To answer the second question first, I have asked the restaurant owner to find you a tourist guide. Someone reliable and trustworthy. Someone who knows this area well. He is to go with you everywhere. Even at night. You have to promise me never to go anywhere alone.'

'I promise. I promise.'

'Now the first question. We know that there are bandit groups. What we want to find out is their connection to Tombouctou. How many groups. Where their bases are likely to be. Other roads and tracks. If they are out there, where are the wells and *gueltas*, oases. They need water. This is the Sahara after all. You must get us geographical information. If we are going to try and rescue David and Moussa, we have to know where these bandits are. We need to be confident, no, dead sure, about their location. Time must be running out.'

There was quiet as the missing men's names turned everyone reflective and subdued; the planning and anticipation for a moment suppressed.

The restaurant owner came over to their table. 'Monsieur, the guide you wanted? Mohamed is here.'

Whitey stood up.

'Marie, help Tecwwa get her few things together. Get mine ready too. Salim and I will talk to the guide, make sure that we are happy with him. We'll also sort the *gendarme* and the other two men out as well. With some money. And that they are okay with the new arrangements.'

The transport ferry chugged slowly across the Niger river. Standing next to his vehicle, Whitey pensively watched the river activity; animals drinking at the water edges, the on-board hawkers and traders, fishermen shouting greetings and offering their catch as they passed by.

Only he really understood what they were trying to do. It was deadly serious; to operate beyond the law, obtain information in such demanding and unknown circumstances. Circumvent governments and authorities, and yet still remain secretive. Nobody could be trusted where there was illicit money to be made. That was why he was so sure they had to split up. Why he, of all of them, had to go to ground, away from prying eyes and ears.

And only when he was ready, when the facts and intelligence were sound, would a rescue mission be attempted. Even then, he would still keep the final details to himself.

Marie had hugged him tightly, whispered in his ear when he left, 'Whatever happens in the future, you are, and will be, the only man for me.' She knew that her husband would give his life to find and save his friend.

What she did not know were the words also uttered by huge Salim just after. 'I may be a big man but your Marie will never see, not know I am always protecting her. But I will, with my life if necessary, in honour of trying to save David and my brother.'

Whitey was under no illusions about the difficulties. Before leaving, as a last attempt he and Tecwwa had gone back to the Mayors office. The bureaucrat had been courteous but trying to get anything out of him was almost impossible.

Blandly officious, he offered nothing. In response to Whitey's more pointed questions, the only answer was, 'The Minister in Bamako is dealing with a situation.'

Whitey tried to probe further, but the man would not budge. He refused to even divulge the names of any officials. 'The matter is confidential and secret.'

But there was something. As the Mayor turned his back on them to take a telephone call, there was a small detail which could not escape the white man's sharp eyesight.

Scrawled on the Mayors desk-pad were notes and words and telephone numbers. There were little drawings and doodles. And slanted in a corner of the pad, Whitey could just make something out.

The figures made no sense, but even upside down he could read the writing

David Cooper/Afrique due Sud/Angleterre?????

Chapter 26
Tempest

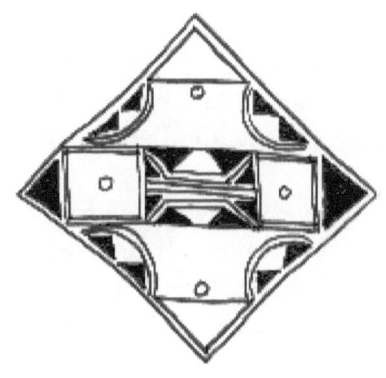

A sound like nothing he had ever heard before. A thrumming, swishing noise that started far off, like a big sea; wave sets that die down slightly, then come back in ever-increasing velocity and sequence.

David could hear his canvas shelter flapping and thrashing about. It was the same with those of his captors. Above the commotion men were shouting, tent pegs being hammered down. Nobody bothered with his, not even to re-tighten the guy lines.

No longer like an ocean now, the wind was gathering force. Though not the same, it reminded him of stampeding animals; half-wild horses on the Mongolian steppes; the great two million strong wildebeest migration and crossing of the Grumeti River in the Serengeti.

One heard it from afar and when it drew near, the sound overtook and drowned you, made you into something insignificant and irrelevant.

And then the dry thunder was upon them, a wild swirling tempest of wind and dust. In a flash his shelter was torn loose, violently hanging to a remaining peg still intact in the ground. With his bound hands and feet tied together, David half rolled, half scuttled crab-like to lie upon the flapping canvas. With a feeble double-armed movement he tried to wrap himself in it, endeavouring to cover his face from the sand. Even the blindfold could not keep the biting grit out.

The weather had been strange that day, starting still, followed by a coolness that seemed to drift off the dunes. With his faculties so altered by not being able to see, his sense of smell and hearing were steadily becoming more acute. Hours earlier, he had perceived the weather changing.

On and on the wind raged. When it lulled slightly, David could hear other noises. Kitchen utensils and debris being blown about, sheep and goats bleating forlornly as they huddled down in their enclosure.

Lying there with the sand flurries slowly covering him, he willed himself into his skull, withdrew into his lizard mind. Mentally he knew where to go. He told himself it was not about survival, it was more than that; he had to maintain self-control, be patient, stave off madness.

During the first few days out here in the Sheikh's camp, uppermost in his thoughts was to see again. Occasionally, when he dozed, the blindfold would slip slightly, loosen a little. But every morning Ahmed would re-fasten it and check that the ropes binding his arms and ankles were still secure.

But David also knew there was more to it than that. There would come a point where internally he would physically break, vital organs damaged beyond repair. This he could not control.

What would happen if his captors did not keep him fed or, more importantly, hydrated properly? When, on the most fearsome of hot days, heatstroke would hit, his body temperature rising away to take him into agonising death.

Could he continually hold his sanity intact? How often could he force his mind into hibernation until something happened; a chance to escape, release or rescue?

He just had to. And he had to believe that something would happen.

But who, and how and when?

Chapter 27
Baaba (Father)

'This is your white man?' The greeting ceremony abandoned at his surprise in seeing Tecwwa again.

The old nomad stood outside his hut, his three wives solemnly in line next to him, the youngest heavily pregnant.

'No, this is another man. He would like to confer with you.'

'This man comes to speak to me in Haribomo!'

'Yes, Baaba.'

'Then we must sit, not stand around like trees.'

In response to a movement of his hand, the middle-aged wife brought out low three-legged stools. Then she disappeared into the hut, returning with a pail of clean water.

Whitey washed his hands and face, Tecwwa her hands only. The veil and headscarf remained in place.

Two calabashes were produced for them to drink out of, one with beer, the other containing watery, slightly fermented, milk.

The man was curious. From underneath his large conical straw and leather hat, his eyes were alert and penetrating.

'Father, this white man speaks none of our languages. You will permit me to translate?'

'Of course. My wives cannot. There is no-one else.'

Whitey looked at the old Fulani; instinctively he knew that Tecwwa's judgement was sound. This was a man who could be depended upon, a man who relished trust. This was a man comfortable in his way of life, a man self-reliant and confident.

'Tell him this,' Whitey said to Tecwwa. 'Tell him that we

believe David is the missing man, the man being held to ransom. Tell him that David is like my brother, but more close. And tell him that to you, David is your fire. Without it you cannot live.'

Carefully Tecwwa translated, her voice shaking slightly.

'Now tell him that we have come back to him for assistance. He must know that you trust him, and you trust me. Tell him also that he honoured you by looking after you, and for that I respect and thank him too.'

The nomad listened carefully, said nothing, his face gravely formal.

'Let him know that we have tried to talk to the mayor in Tombouctou. We believe that the mayor is untruthful. He will not help us.'

There were a few quick and straight words in response.

Tecwwa spoke, 'Baaba agrees. In this country few can be trusted. He also asks, what do you want him to do?'

'This is what we want to know. There are three vital things. How many bandit groups operate in the area around Tombouctou? Any information on their bases? And has anyone seen a white man with one of these groups?'

Tecwwa turned back to Whitey. 'Baaba here says. This land, this country very big. Only nomads travel all areas. Nomads know how easy it is to hide. Maybe difficult to get true story.'

The white man nodded in agreement. 'Yes, but just one piece of information, the right information, could save your David's life.'

In less than half an hour a plan had been worked out. Baaba had rejected the idea of moving his herds and flocks northwards. He opted to take a few sheep to the market instead. This meant that he could move quickly, able to circulate in Tombouctou within a day.

It was also agreed that Tecwwa and Whitey would stay behind, camp in Haribomo. A rendezvous point on the Niger River was determined.

'Give me three days,' were the old man's words.

He was already gone with one of his young sons accompanying him. He knew exactly what was required.

The shot and ricochet died in a diminishing scream.

'Show me how, please,' a quiet voice asked

Whitey lowered his rifle and flipped the safety catch. Tecwwa stood behind him.

'You want to learn to shoot?'

'Yes.'

He didn't even think twice. Filling the magazine, he re-loaded and handed the CR-21 assault rifle to her. She found it surprisingly light.

'Hold the butt to your shoulder. Not too tight. Just firm. With your right eye look through the sight. Can you see two horizontal marks?'

'Yes.'

'And an inverted V.'

'A what?'

An upside-down V mark.'

'Yes.'

With his finger Whitey pointed. 'Can you see that dark rock? About a hundred metres away. There are some bigger white ones around it.'

Tecwwa nodded. 'I see, it's quite far away.'

'Yes, that is your target. But this rifle is a killing machine and the bullet is live. So what am I telling you?'

'The target is live too.'

'Yes, it is your enemy. It is responsible for kidnapping David. And imagine it can shoot back too.'

She took a deep breath.

'Release the safety, like this,' Whitey instructed. 'Now just relax. Aim the sights, those marks, straight. Stand still, breathe light, shallow. Then squeeze the trigger gently. Just feel it back.'

She fired. Whitey couldn't be certain, but he thought that it was only marginally wide.

'Let's go a little closer.'

Once again, he helped her prepare. 'Make sure the rifle is firm to your shoulder. Aim, now ease the trigger back.'

This time she didn't miss; a shard of dark brown rock exploded away in splinters.

Tecwwa murmured, '*Khanzeer*, die.'

Marie had had enough of ancient and dusty old Islamic manuscripts stacked high on shelves which for years were never cleaned or dusted. From previous generations and times, even to the present, the works were a treasure house for academics. But to her, who neither understood nor really wanted to understand them, the writings were impressive but boring.

And she was tired, too. Late nights out eating and dancing with the locals, fending off groping hands in grimy *shebeens*; her scalp itching under its new false hairstyle. She wished Whitey would return.

There was time to visit one more place, after that, she was going back to the *auberge* to sleep.

'I want to see the house of explorer Laing.'

The guide, Mohamed looked at her wearily. Charging around with Marie had taken its toll on him as well.

'Madame, maybe tomorrow .... ?'

'No, let's go there now. According to my guide-book it's nearby.'

Slowly he spread the old diagram out. 'As a young man, my grandfather travelled with him!'

Looking at her notes and then at the curator, Marie judged him to be in his eighties. A man trying to preserve something old and interesting; a passage in time, an era that would surely end when he died.

'Laing was a very difficult man.'

'In what way?'

'He was arrogant. Many people of the desert not like him.'

'And he explored this way?'

'Yes, Madame.' With a wavering finger he drew an imaginary trail. 'That was the way he came to Tombouctou. He left the same way, but was killed by nomads near Araouane. In Christian year 1826.'

Despite her fatigue, a resonance went through her head, a recall of what Whitey might want.

'The roads in and out of Tombouctou are still the same. The same as on Laing's sketch?'

'To the east and west they are still the same. To the south there are many. It depends on the rain and where the River flows.'

'And the north?'

'These days the road is different. Not quite the same here. But before, when the great trading parties passed through, it went from here to here.'

Marie knew then she had to know more. She sensed that there was some significance, couldn't quite put her finger on it.

'So this new road also goes to Araouane.'

'Yes, it goes this way.'

'And the old route, the one the traders and explorers used?'

'It is this one to the left side,' and he drew the imaginary trail again.

'Is it still there?'

The curator looked doubtful. 'Some parts maybe, probably you can only see it when the sky is clear and the moon is bright.'

Slowly Salim ate from the large bowl in front of him. With his massive fingers he formed the couscous into delicate small balls which he dipped into a spicy chilli sauce.

Around him sat half a dozen young boys, sipping from cool drinks Salim had brought them. All day they had been watching as he went through his training regime. In the morning he had done stretching exercises followed by free weights; huge rocks in curls and presses, followed by push-ups and dips. Later some of them ran with him, ten kilometres along the road towards

Akédkod and then back. And after all of this, what impressed them the most was how in practice he turned their local heroes over. One after the other he had his opponents on their backs, pinned down in the sand.

One of the wrestlers was a muscular heavyweight who stayed behind talking to Salim about grappling and technique. They arranged to meet later.

The man was becoming garrulous as the effects of a third large beer took place.

'I am in the *militaire*,' he said.

'Hm, *militaire*,' Salim repeated.

'Yes, I have just been promoted. To sergeant.'

'You must be very good,' Salim murmured.

'Yes, our unit is Special Force. Some of us, the best, have been to France for training. And the French commandos have come here too. To work with us.'

'They are here now?'

'No, no, about six months ago they moved on. To Burkina then, I think, maybe to Senegal.'

Salim sipped his Fanta orange. *There is information in this man*, he could hear Whitey's voice in his ear. *Try and obtain it.*

'And now, what are you doing?'

'We patrol here, we patrol there. Sometimes we have fun,' the man grinned lopsidedly.

'Fun?'

'Last month we had fun. There were fools from Chad, gun runners. We caught them near Ti-In Essako. The poor camels were so laden, couldn't run anywhere.'

In response to a signal from Salim, the bar owner opened another beer for the soldier.

'Heh, heh,' he gurgled.

'There is something more funny?' Salim asked.

'I don't know why they call them gun runners. Only one may possibly run again; the rest have finished their race. Their race to the Creator.'

'I am surprised that the French army still comes here,' Salim remarked casually.

'Oh yes, from Foreign Legion days. Many, many years they come, here. There are run-down bases and disused airfields all around. Even now some bases are still in good condition, still being used'

'These are all around Tombouctou?'

'No, no, my friend,' the soldier was starting to slur. 'In Algeria, Niger, Burkina Faso, Tunisia, Morocco and other countries.'

'Here in Mali?'

'Oh yes, even near Tombouctou there are two.'

Salim knew that he had heard something important.

Whitey brought the vehicle to a halt, pulled off the track into the meagre shade of a few small thorn-bushes. The air was searingly hot, made worse by the cattle flies which were smothering and interminable.

'I think this is meeting place for nomad,' Tecwwa said to Whitey. 'Down there. This is how he explained it.'

Across the river Whitey thought he could see someone, or rather two people. Training his binoculars on them, the old Fulani nomad and his young son came into focus.

'They are on the other side,' he stated, 'But it's too early, I don't want to cross now. Not in the daylight. We must keep a low profile, as few people as possible must see us.'

'Let me go,' Tecwwa said. 'No-one will know who I am.'

He watched her black-clad figure negotiate with a fisherman. With her face fully covered, nobody would be able to identify her.

Within minutes she was in a small dugout canoe being conveyed to the other side.

An hour later Tecwwa was back, accompanied by the Fulani and the boy. She pulled her veil down, was clearly livid, her dark eyes flashing and angry.

'Baaba knows something, but won't tell me!'

Whitey placated her. 'Calm down, just be patient! He probably wants to share what he knows with both of us. And he's also curious, wants to know what we plan to do next.'

'Hmmh!'

Deliberately Baaba knocked out his pipe, filled and lit it. He began speaking.

'This is what the people are saying.'

'Which people?'

'Slowly, my sister, I know you are anxious for news.'

Smoke seeped from his nostrils as he exhaled.

'The herdsmen here are saying that there is only one bandit group in this area. There was another, but they say that group has moved far away. Now have a base near a place called Agadez.'

He waited while Tecwwa translated to Whitey, who commented, 'Agadez is in Niger, in the far northeast.'

'The herdsmen are also saying that the group which is still operating here comes from Mauritania.'

Whitey spoke to Tecwwa. 'Ask him, nicely,' and he grinned, 'to please tell us the important part.'

She didn't have to, Baaba was already talking. 'What you want to know is this. The Maur group has a white man in captivity. One herdsman saw them when they were travelling.'

'Travelling where to?'

'They were seen putting fuel into two vehicles. They were going north. To a place in the north.'

'In Mauritania?'

'No, no, still in Mali.'

'Where is it?'

158

The old man shook his head, 'I have never been to that place. But the people here say it is near a village on the way to the salt mines.'

'What is the name of the village?'

'I am not sure, but it is the only village along that road. And the road is very, very long and nearly straight all the way.'

Whitey stood, went and fetched a map from his car. He opened it. 'Ask him to show us where he thinks it is.'

Baaba shook his head negatively. 'I cannot read, don't need map. In Mali I use the land, that which I can see, as my map.'

Tecwwa looked frustrated.

'There is one more thing. There is one man who is go-between.'

'Go-between?'

'Yes.'

'Who is he?'

'The go-between is a *Marabout*. The bandit leader will only talk to him, will only negotiate through him with government. Will not deal with anyone else.'

'Do you know the *Marabout's* name?'

'No. Of him there is little information.'

'What is he negotiating for?'

The old man looked surprised, almost as if he thought the question too naive.

'The release price for the white man!'

Whitey looked out across the landscape, the broad expanse of the slow moving river absorbing his thoughts; it was like watching the sea. Somehow the motion of water in nature made him thoughtful, meditative, plans seemed to come easily then.

'This is what we are going to do. We need to meet with the others, see what they've been able to find out. Baaba must help us with one more thing.'

'What shall I ask him?' Tecwwa said.

'Two of us will walk into Tombouctou from here. Tonight.

It's not far, less than ten kilometres. One must stay back to look after the car.'

'And?'

'You must stay behind with the boy. And with my rifle. The old man goes with me.'

'Why must he go with you?'

'Firstly if there is information, enough for us to move on, presumably to the north, I will need him to buy some camels. To help us bring more supplies back here to our car.'

'Why don't we just put the car on a barge and cross over to Tombouctou?'

'Because we will be seen. Someone will talk. Tell the authorities.'

'But you will be seen!'

Whitey grinned. 'No I won't.'

Tecwwa looked perplexed. 'I don't understand.'

Baaba just shook his head, could not stop laughing.

Tecwwa's spare robe was a bit tight across the shoulders, but otherwise it fitted perfectly. Walking next to the old Fulani in the dark, Whitey was completely concealed; from head to toe; a full veil, and with Tecwwa's leather sandals loosely buckled to his feet.

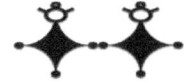

Chapter 28
Burial Ground

'Please be quiet, my darling,' the hard calloused hand across her mouth was firm yet still gentle. 'Don't be scared, *cariad*.'

The intense fright dissipated as Marie realised who it was. She knew those hands like those of no other.

'Whitey?'

'Yes, it's me. Put the light on.'

'There's no power. Let me get my torch. There's a kerosene lamp and matches on the table.'

It didn't take long. The room was soon dimly illuminated.

'Ooh-la-la, Whitey, what have you been up to? Have you gone through a life changing experience?' She started to giggle, but Whitey put his finger to her lips.

'Ssh, do you know where Salim is staying?'

'Yes. But I haven't seen him though. He left me a little sketch of where his room is. I think it's just around the corner.'

'Dress quickly. There's an old man outside the door. He can be trusted. Take him with you. Go and fetch Salim now. Bring him back here.'

'Whitey, you might be wearing the wrong clothes, but one thing first!' Her kiss was lingering and heartfelt.

Whitey had washed and changed by the time Marie and Salim returned. The giant looked pleased to see him too. Four days had passed. They all had information to share.

The old Fulani nomad looked around, pulling a threadbare carpet into a corner of the room. He lay down, and in an instant was asleep.

'Where is Tecwwa, Whitey?'

'She is on the southern side of the river, guarding the Land

Cruiser.'

'Guarding our car! With what? A stick!'

Whitey smiled grimly. 'No, she has one of my rifles.'

'Can she shoot? She'll be too scared to use it,' Marie exclaimed.

'I don't think so.'

'What?'

'Let me put it this way. She can't miss.' Tecwwa had practiced with greater dexterity and more natural proficiency than he had seen in most men. Her eye for a target was phenomenal.

'Oh, and another thing,' Whitey went on, 'Tecwwa is fuming. Furious with everyone other than ourselves. Nobody else better upset her. Our vehicle is definitely safe.'

Marie's eyes were large and incredulous. 'And now?'

'Let's go through what we know.'

'Must I make notes?' Marie interrupted.

'No, no. Let's keep it in our heads.' Whitey held up his hand, fingers extending one by one. 'Firstly there is only one bandit group in the Tombouctou area. Secondly, they have a white man hostage. Thirdly, they operate from a base in the north. Fourth, the base is near a village on the road to the salt mines. And five, there is someone, a *Marabout*, acting as a negotiator.'

'What is a *Marabout*?' Marie asked.

'It is Muslim holy man,' Salim interrupted before Whitey could respond.

'Yes, you are right. But many of them have turned fundamentalist now. They have become hard-line activists. Recruiting students for the radical *madrassas*. Trying to extort money from wherever they can.'

The light from the lamp shone flickeringly across their faces. Whitey went on. 'The information we have, we really knew before, as rumours, as bones, but now I am willing to believe it. What we need to do is put some meat onto the bones.'

Salim's deep voice spoke. 'What I know is this. Gun runners were caught and killed near the Niger border. These bandits must have loaded the weapons from a base somewhere. Maybe flown in to an old airfield for onward transport. Transport by camels, as we have heard of before.'

'I wonder how many old airfields and bases there are around. Could be quite a few; from the colonial days, for troop movements,' Whitey mused aloud.

'No,' Salim was assertive. 'There are only two. One is far away to the west. I think it is not that one.'

'There is one in the north, Salim?'

'Yes. My information is good.'

'Where is it?' Whitey asked.

'That answer I do not know. I could not ask, might have drawn suspicion.'

'What about the *Marabout*? Anybody heard of him?' Whitey looked at them, but Marie and Salim both shook their heads, faces blank. He spread his map out on the table and drew it closer.

'Where can that base be?'

'Let's ask him, Whitey,' Salim pointed to the nomad Baaba on the floor.

'I tried already, but he doesn't know. Can't read either.'

'Can't read a map?'

'No.'

'Where can that base be?' Whitey repeated.

As a moth fluttered inquisitively around the lamp, trying to get at the flame, they examined the map. The detail was minimal.

Marie suddenly jumped up. Opening her haversack, she took her camera out of its case.

'There's a bell!'

'What?'

'A bell, a bell, it rings,' she cried. 'I can hear it.'

'What the hell are you talking about?' Whitey and Salim looked at each other expressively.

Marie switched the camera on; went through the digital modes in playback. Intently she looked at each picture until she came to the right one.

'Look Whitey, look Salim, look closely.'

From over her shoulder, the two peered at the photograph.

'It looks like a portion of a map.'

'Yes, it's one of the explorer's maps. Heinrich Barth, who explored here in the 1850s.'

'Can you make the detail bigger?'

She enhanced the image as much as she could. 'Look at the big map and then at my picture.' Carefully the men studied what were in front of them, trying to puzzle out what Marie was showing them.

'There is something that's not on our modern map,' Whitey remarked.

'Yes!' Marie said excitedly.

'There's also some faint writing.'

'Yes!'

'It's too small to read.'

'Wait.' Again she rummaged in her bag. She handed her reading glasses over to Whitey. 'Use these like a magnifying glass.'

Now he could make out the words, 'I think it's written in German, translates into

"*large salt pan.*"

'Show me the other pictures you took. Of this old map.'

As Marie scrolled through the images, Whitey neatly pencilled in the position of the salt pan on his larger current map.

'So, what does this tell us?'

'Whitey, I know, I know!' Marie had her hand in the air, like an eager schoolgirl wanting to answer a question.

He knew the answer too, but with a little smile allowed her to speak.

'Look.' With her finger she prodded at the map. 'Look, all sand dunes everywhere. Look it says *Erg*, here and here and here. But this is a salt pan. Long, flat hard edges; just the place to build an airstrip in the middle of nowhere. For patrolling by air the vast French territories in colonial times.'

'Yes, I agree,' Whitey said, 'and there is something more. Something our sleeping friend told us. The base is near a village en-route to the salt mines. On the only road! The only village! This pan could be a few kilometres from Araouane!'

'No, wait, maybe a bit further.' Carefully, Whitey scaled the distance off. 'Probably more like twenty to twenty five kilometres.'

'We can drive there and go and look,' Marie said.

Both the men shook their heads. This time, Salim spoke. 'Too dangerous, Madame. This is big business; bad people trying to make money in a bad way. If we leave Tombouctou going on that road, we will definitely be stopped. By police or by military. Important people will want a cut of the ransom.'

Whitey looked out of the window. Slowly, it was getting lighter. Already there were noises, people coughing as they arose, donkeys braying; from the nearest mosque, the muezzin had already made his plaintive second call to prayer.

'This is what we'll do. Marie, continue today with your sight-seeing as you have been doing. Then pay your guide up to date. Tell him you want to rest for a day or two. That you're waiting for me to get back.'

'Ok, Whitey. There is one museum I haven't been to yet. I'll go there,' and she sighed dramatically.

'Salim, do your training as normal. But you must try and get us another piece of information. I know it's risky, but we have to be sure. I'll give you money for a bribe if necessary.'

'You want me to get the name of the *Marabout*, find out who and where he is.'

'That would be a bonus. No, what we really need is confirmation of that base. We can't try and find it unless we are certain it exists.'

'I understand,' the big man agreed.

'Madame, you are interested in these old explorers?'

'*Oui, oui,* Monsieur, I am doing studies for another degree, distance study in France.'

Marie did not know why she told the white lie, but the caretaker seemed so interested. He was an earnest studious man of about forty, an academic who had under achieved, probably due to lack of money, or ambition, or both. She managed to keep the conversation superficial and ever so slightly flirtatious.

'I am particularly interested in the even older travellers. The great caravan trading routes. North-South, East–West. I have heard so many fascinating stories since I've been in Tombouctou.'

'Oh, yes Madame, there are even some interesting ones from more recent times.'

'Really,' and she raised her eyebrows in query, shook her upper body slightly.

His eyes glistened salaciously. 'About seventy years ago the French military needed an airfield. So they found a site which they levelled and compacted, white washed stones to mark it out and raised a flagpole. Do you know what happened next?'

'*Non, Monsieur,* please tell me,' and she touched his arm lightly. Her thoughts raced, could this be that vital missing jigsaw piece?

'The first time they were going to land a plane, they couldn't.'

'Why not?'

'Walking right across the middle of the new landing strip were Tuareg nomads with flocks of camels, sheep and goats. And following behind were their servants, Bella and others, all with their livestock. Maybe two thousand animals.'

'And then?'

'The poor pilot couldn't land. His fuel was low so he tried to land closer to a nearby village. But the terrain was rough and very sandy. The minute the plane hit the ground, it somersaulted and disintegrated.'

'The pilot was killed?'

'Yes, Madame. You see, without realising it, the French built that airfield on a trading route. One that had been in use for so many centuries.'

Marie knew she had to keep the story going, fiddled with a button on her blouse, inviting his eyes to her cleavage. 'I suppose that horrible accident closed the airfield down.'

'*Non, Non, Madame,*' he answered looking downward, eyeing her voluptuous pose. 'They stationed a small permanent unit there to prevent the situation happening again. And also over the years the caravans dwindled. Now nothing passes there anymore.'

'This was in Mali?'

'Oh, yes, *Madame*, not far from here. Well.... in our terms not far.'

'In the east or west?'

'*Non, Madame,* in the north, slightly west, near Araouane.'

Salim looked downcast when he came in that evening. 'I have nothing to report,' he said glumly.

'Don't worry, my friend,' Whitey said, 'we have important information. Tell him, Marie, tell him what the museum caretaker told you.'

Quickly, she related her news.

'Now we are going to move. Salim, go and fetch your things plus the extra supplies you have bought. Bring it all back here.'

'Where is the Fulani Baaba?' The big man asked.

'He is out at the back. With two camels to carry everything. We have been waiting for you. Marie has paid for the room. We need to return to Tecwwa. It is time to go.'

They had to take a longer route in order to get back to where Tecwwa was camped. Finding a shallow spot in the river had been difficult, especially at night. The camels would not cross where the water was more than knee-deep.

In the dark, as they drew nearer, they could see Tecwwa looking in their direction; the blue-grey sheen of the rifle in her arms clearly visible. She was wide-awake and fully alert.

'She is not alone,' Whitey whispered.

Next to him, Salim stopped. 'I cannot see anyone else.'

'I can smell them,' the white man answered softly.

'Smell them?'

'I can always smell the mixture of blood and fear.'

They drew closer so that Tecwwa could see who they were. She lowered the rifle and came over to them. The two women embraced; Tecwwa looked confident and composed.

In the shadows away from the fire, Whitey could see two men

168

trussed up together. Salim joined him and they examined the hapless pair.

'They are Hausa people, from Niger,' Salim said. 'They must have sneaked up on her. Or threatened her in some way.'

'Yes, but she was waiting for them. Look at what she has done.' Whitey pointed to their arms. The pain must have been excruciating, for Tecwwa had shot them; two bullets each, shattering not only both left and right collarbones, but their shoulder blades as well. They were tied together, back to back, in total agony.

'We need to move fast. Before it gets light. Cross the river where we brought the camels through. And then up into the desert where we can hide out.' Whitey was talking as he worked, loading the additional baggage, carefully securing everything into place.

'Tecwwa, tell Baaba, we are really grateful for his help. The camels he may keep, they are his payment.'

She moved over to the nomad, spoke to him quietly. Baaba asked her where they were going. 'We are moving north, we are going to find my man.'

The old Fulani nodded thoughtfully. 'When we first spoke, when we met in the Dogon County and I agreed to help you, do you remember what I said.'

'I do. You said: *what could three people do to free my David, that the Government and Military could not do.*'

'Yes, that is what I said. But now I think differently. With you, with that Elephant,' pointing to Salim, 'and with that wild, clever man leading, there may be a chance.'

Whitey came over just as he finished speaking. 'Ask Baaba that I would like him to do one more thing for us. If he will agree.'

'What do want from him?' Tecwwa asked.

'Those two, the Hausa that you shot. If we tie them to the camels, will he free them in a day or two's time? Somewhere south. We will be far away by then.'

The old nomad agreed. In an amazed voice he uttered to Tecwwa, 'not only is he wild and clever, but cunning like a menacing *nboodi*.'

Marie had never been so hot in her life. Even under the makeshift tarpaulin shelter the temperature had to be over 50°C. Tecwwa had given her a spare robe to wear, the one Whitey had used. She wore it without underclothes, her Tuareg friend was doing the same.

Sitting in the shade, Salim was suffering as well. His huge body stoically still.

Only Whitey seemed unaffected by the heat as he worked through his list of notes. He had a plan for each day ahead; how far they would travel, how much water they were allowed each, what they would eat, even an allocation of guns and bullets.

The vehicle was re-packed with the same care; weapons and tools always easily accessible.

As closely as he could, Whitey had marked up the old North – South trading route on his modern map, working from Marie's photographs and her recollected conversations with the various museum curators.

'We'll mainly travel at night, mostly without lights. We need to find that old way as soon as possible,' he told them. 'We'll try and alternate, sometimes use the trail, sometimes use the road to Araouane. If anyone has heard of us, is trying to find us, we need ....'

'Whitey, nobody travels in Mali at night. It is too dangerous,' Tecwwa interjected.

'I know. But we have to keep a low profile. And because other people won't travel at night there's also less chance of us being seen.'

'How far do you think we have to go?' Marie asked.

'If that salt pan is where we think it is, about two hundred and eighty kilometres.' Whitey could sense her thought process.

'About five or six days travel. We have to be really cautious.'

Marie's shoulders slumped, but only for a moment. Then she perked up and looked at the others squarely. 'If I start to complain, even once, tell me to shut up. Just kick my plump French *derrière*!'

'There is one more thing,' Whitey looked at Tecwwa as he spoke. 'We will not be able to rescue David alone.'

He could see Salim look at him quizzically. Somehow they both knew it was unlikely that Moussa was still alive. Unless he had gotten away. But there had been no report of him from the very beginning of their quest.

'Araouane must be a Tuareg village. Probably only a few people live there. We will need to try and recruit one or two men. You will have to talk to them.'

'I understand. The Tuareg like to hunt.'

'But if the village is getting money from the bandits, we'll have a problem,' Whitey stated.

Tecwwa nodded. 'I do not know that place, but all Tuareg are connected. There will be those whose honour it is to help my family name. These are ties deeper than money.'

Steadily circling Tombouctou, Whitey drove slowly through the dry, scrubby semi-desert until they crossed the rutted narrow road heading north. By his reckoning they were twenty kilometres north of the town.

'I think we'll use the road for the next few hours, try and get some distance under our belts.'

He stopped the vehicle. The engine's clicking and cooling sounded loud in the still night.

Quickly he and Salim assembled the sub-machine gun from its storage box on the roof. He clipped a rifle into a bracket in the roof cab above his head and handed another to Tecwwa.

'Tecwwa, you will sit here. Hold the rifle over your left shoulder.' On the bonnet, Whitey had built a temporary seat with a leather strap handle for her to hold on to. Two more leather straps had been fastened on the front bumper, stirrups for her feet to hook into. 'You must always wear these,' and he handed Tecwwa a pair of clear safety glasses. 'Keep your headscarf wrapped around as well. Never, even for a moment, take them off when we're driving. An insect or stone in your eye could blind you!'

'What am I going to do?' Marie queried.

'You are going to record our journey and help navigate. Make notes and sketches. Every bump and turn. Work out our fuel consumption, kilometre by kilometre.'

Marie nodded, 'I agree, this will be important.'

'You know why this is important?'

'Whitey, we have to get back too!'

'Yes, now let's get going. This is where the fun starts.'

That first night was strangely anti-climatic. Progress was slow without lights, occasionally they lost the road. When this happened Whitey would immediately stop until the two men had found it again. By four o'clock in the morning the speedometer indicated that they had covered nearly half the journey. Now it was time to rest up. Carefully he pulled off the road, heading well away from it. The desert felt firm under the tyres; he knew that the fine sand particles bound better when the air was still cool.

All the time they had made on the first night, was lost during the second. Whitey knew the signs; it was similar to the east weather in Namibia that he had experienced in his youth.

After another scorching day in the open desert; he warned the others what was coming.

'Tonight we stay put, batten down the hatches.'

Tecwwa looked crestfallen. 'But Whitey, let's at least carry on until the wind starts. Then we can stop.'

'No, I'm sorry; it's just not worth it. You'll soon see why.'

He made them store everything away, cover and tie all their possessions down securely. They turned their enclosure into a bunker, digging the sand out so that they could comfortably crouch down, well below ground level. Across it they stretched the tarpaulin into a taut flat roof securely lashed and pegged down. Their weapons were fastidiously wrapped and stowed in the car.

And Whitey was just as particular with their vehicle. All the larger vents were plugged with cloth; wherever dust could penetrate was either sealed with grease or soap or masking tape. He did the same with the radiator grille, carefully and tightly covering it over.

Now they could hear what was coming. A far off low roar slowly building; and they could see what was coming too. A rush of fine dust, followed by billows of sand and grit.

The others had never experienced a sand storm of this magnitude before, even Tecwwa, who had grown up in a desert habitat. In the stifling bunker the two women curled up together, their faces covered with damp cloths. Salim had his covered as well.

In all the years she had been with him, Marie had come to realise that Whitey was different. She loved him so much but now it was more. He was so physically tough and resourceful. Her awe of him made her feel safe.

And now there was this fury. This wind of violence. For the first time in three days she watched Whitey settle down, instantly asleep. And sleep soundly for hours. Secure in his knowledge of the elements. This was a time when he did not have to worry about, or protect them. The environment was now protecting them all.

The stillness and the brightness woke them.

Pulling the tarpaulin cover back which had been their vital

protection from the night-sandstorm, Whitey stood above them holding three mugs of coffee.

After the fury of the wind it was now so quiet, the air crystal clear and bracing; the boundless open sky a brilliant azure blue. The desert heat in that early morning had been blown away.

'How long have you been up?' Marie asked blearily.

'About four hours, as soon as the wind died down.'

'Four hours! It's only eight o'clock now! And in the dark, what have you been doing?'

Marie could see that look in him again. Whitey had rested and was refreshed. The predatory instinct pulsated in him; he was holding it tightly under control.

'I've been busy. Made you all breakfast. More importantly I have also found something.

'What have you found?'

'I'll show you when you're up.'

The three looked a little sheepish as they dusted themselves down and straightened their clothes. Not only had Whitey cleaned and checked the car; their weapons lay ready for use, carefully oiled and prepared. Ammunition neatly placed next to each one. And laid out on the camping table was a spread of freshly boiled eggs which Whitey had already peeled, dates, and a mixture of tinned and fresh fruit salad. Covered by a cloth were small loaves of crusty damper bread just taken off the fire.

Each one absorbed in their own thoughts, they quietly ate their meal. A few beige-coloured wheatears scavenged for crumbs and over a little water that Whitey had poured into a jam-jar lid.

Tecwwa spoke first. 'Whitey, you wanted to show us something.'

'Yes, but we'll tidy and pack up first. It's about two kilometres away. We'll drive there.'

Marie looked surprised. 'You've been that far already.'

'Hmm, yes.'

The others realised that Whitey must have patrolled the immediate surrounding area on foot. Probably as soon as he had arisen.

'These are human bones!' Tecwwa exclaimed.

Whitey pointed. 'There are more, come with me.'

In a small shallow dip were the remnants of skeletons. A few ribs still attached to breastbones; tibiae, pieces of bleached femora, even a few skulls. More unidentifiable fragments lay strewn around.

'What is this place?' Marie asked, sounding frightened.

'I think the bones are very old,' Whitey replied. He examined their faces. 'Remember the maps?'

The others looked puzzled.

'Remember the word *Erg*?'

'Ye-yes,' Marie muttered hesitantly.

'*Erg* means more than sand dune. It also means shifting sands.'

'You think the wind uncovered the bones?'

'Oh, yes,' Whitey looked nonchalant.

'Come on, Whitey. Stop playing games with us!'

'Burial place,' Salim's deep voice intoned.

'Ah, yes, but for whom? There is no settlement near here. Not for a hundred kilometres in either direction at least. Probably more,' Whitey emphasized.

This time it was Tecwwa who was hesitant, but she knew the answer. 'I think .... maybe burial ground for nomads and trading people. People who used North-South route. From olden times.'

Whitey grinned, '*Dewch, dilynwch fi, fy anwyliaid.* Follow me, my dears.'

Quickly he led the way; through a vee between two low dunes and then left sharply up a higher one. With the vista open below and beyond them and the air so still and clear, they could seemingly see forever to the horizon.

And just as clearly they could see the wide, wending path. Through the binoculars it looked so obvious. Hundreds, probably nearer to thousands, of years of use had shaped the way through the landscape. At places where dunes had advanced and encroached, drifts of sand spilled over. But the sandy trail, used by so many people for so long, lay before them.

'I think that if we had camped in a different place or if the light was different, like later in the day, it wouldn't be so easy to see,' Whitey said. 'The wind has settled everything down. No dust, no haze or anything at the moment.'

For a while, the four of them all stood there.

'I think we can take a chance, follow this old route for a while,' Whitey announced, 'and try and make up for the time we lost yesterday.

'In the daylight? Somebody might see us?' Marie asked.

'Mm, I don't think so. Anyone out this way will probably use the road. Especially if they were caught in the sandstorm too.'

He went on. 'Wait here. Salim and I will check first. See how firm the terrain is.'

For more than an hour the two women waited, talking quietly between themselves. Marie was burning with curiosity; she wanted to know about the Hausa. Why Tecwwa had shot them. So far Tecwwa had kept it to herself, had not spoken of the confrontation at all.

Yet even now, Marie could not ask the question. Instead they conversed about other things, of their journey so far, of the heat and wind from the previous night. Wondering what lay ahead for them.

Together they looked northwards; in the far distance Whitey and Salim could be seen returning along the trail.

'We are facing the footsteps of a million ghosts,' Marie murmured.

'We are facing the way to finding my David,' Tecwwa echoed.

Chapter 29
Sheikh Saffah

'What the hell are you?'

David looked around. Ahmed had half-led, half-dragged him across to the Sheikh's tent. Once inside he had been pushed down into a sitting position, only then was the blindfold removed.

The tent was surprisingly well appointed and self contained. Intricately patterned carpets lay spread across the canvas floor. Neatly lined wall hangings covered the side walls; the hangings were filled with Arabic writing. To the rear of the tent was a dividing curtain; David presumed this to be the man's sleeping quarters.

Old and beautifully preserved antique furnishings stood in each corner; a polished samovar and an intricate carved chest of drawers; mounted pairs of huge crossed swords, four sets in all. Everything polished and dust-free.

This was clearly a permanent base and home.

Lounging on leather covered cushions were half a dozen men; the Sheikh and two of his henchmen, a burly man in Malian military uniform, and two others, who seemed to be Muslim priests.

'You will answer when I speak to you,' the man hissed.

'I'm afraid I don't understand your question fully.'

'What is so difficult? Are you British or not?'

'I am a British citizen, but South African by birth. You have taken my passport, you can see from that.'

One of the religious clerics intervened. 'Where does your family live?'

'I have a sister who lives in Australia. That is all.'

'What about the rest? Parents, uncles, cousins? Where are they?'

'My parents passed away some time ago. My sister is my only living relative. She has never married. There is no-one else.'

'No other family! By blood or marriage?' The *Marabout* looked incredulous.

'No,' David replied.

There was a vigorous exchange in Arabic between the cleric and the Sheikh.

The *Marabout* turned to him, his English was harsh and stilted, influenced by a Middle Eastern accent. 'We have demanded the sum of one million dollars for your release. The British government have declined to respond. We have sent the same demand to South Africa. They have responded.'

'In what way?' David asked.

'They have sympathy for your situation, but offer no money for your freedom. But they say that with your written approval any money you have in South Africa can be quickly released, paid over instead.'

He sat there trying to work the situation out. The *Marabout* and his aide appeared to be negotiators; the Malian army man he could only presume was there for face, to pass messages on. Or maybe representing somebody higher up in Government who was on the take too. The Sheikh clearly dealt with no-one directly.

'Your situation is very serious,' the man went on. 'You will not be released without payment being received.'

'My pension and savings are invested in England. What guarantees can you give that if I sign them over, I will be released?'

'The Sheikh is a man of honour. You will be released.'

'There is no honour in him.'

Almost before David had finished speaking, the Sheikh was on him, huge knife at his throat.

'I will kill this *kafir* now.'

The *Marabout* stood and prised him away firmly. 'Then the money we are working for, the time this has all taken, will be wasted.'

'Your *madrassas* want their share, the Malians want their share,' the Sheikh shouted. 'Remember I already have wealth, I don't need a share.'

The *Marabout* remained unperturbed. 'Yes, I agree, but this arrangement has worked well in the past. With the Swiss, with the Italians, and the French. We have all done well.'

As quickly as the anger had risen, it subsided. The Sheikh spoke to one of his men, who silently left the room. There was an immediate reduction in tension. Soon he returned carrying a tray; crystal-cut shot glasses and a tall exquisite Arabian tea pot.

David watched as they drank. Nothing was offered to him. In his weakened state, with his olfactory sense enhanced, the smell of the leaf was so sweet, reminiscent of tea-times shared with Tecwwa. He sat there somnolent and drowsy. Suddenly, something seemed to beat in his head, almost like an internal flash light, a lightning image of her, as if in some way she was nearby. A triggered image gone in an instant.

'I will sign what you need me to.'

With a shaky hand David signed the papers the Sheikh took from the armoire. There were clean standard papers for all the major banking institutions; powers of attorney, bankers drafts and withdrawal forms. There was even a large envelope into which the signed documents were placed.

The meeting was over. There were no handshakes or farewells. Noiselessly, the two clerics and their military accomplice left the room; with them the envelope carefully stowed in a leather satchel. Within minutes a car started up and they were gone. Following a dismissive hand gesture, the henchmen withdrew as well.

'You have a million in your bank accounts?'

'Yes, about that.' David said.

'You are prepared to give me all your money to live?'

'Yes.'

'That is where we are different.'

'Why?'

'Even if I die, I still live. My money, which is far more than yours, will be allocated more wisely.'

David shrugged. 'You are in a position of strength. I have no options. And I disagree with you as well.'

The Sheikh's voice mocked, yet his eyes carried a vicious dangerous anger. 'You choose to disagree with me. I find that very amusing. Tell me why you disagree.'

'A true believer will go on to eternal life, as will a martyr or a *jihadi* if it's in a just and wise cause. But you are a mercenary, a weapons and drug smuggler, a people thief. You will go to continuous fire.'

'That is why I asked what the hell you were,' he launched again. 'You white South Africans have no fear. You are not British. No ordinary European would deign to place the Koran in front of me.'

David felt exhausted, merely the strain of talking had caused the exertion. But he knew it was more than that. Captivity was making him ever weaker; into a third month of poor food, little water and no activity. The only time he had regained some strength was during the camel journey from the Adrar. And that was many weeks ago.

The Sheikh shouted. Ahmed appeared and handed David a glass of water.

'I want to show you something.' From a drawer he removed a large black-framed photograph. Ahmed brought it over to David.

'You went to Sandhurst?'

'Oh yes. It was a reward promised to my father for helping British explorers in the Empty Quarter.'

'You are from Saudi Arabia?'

'Yes, but more than that. I am a Bedouin.'

'What happened at Sandhurst?'

David could see the anger leap into his face again. 'I was their best trainee, the best marksman, the fittest and most clever.'

'What happened then?'

'The bastards didn't recognise what they had in me. Wouldn't commission or promote me.'

'Maybe they did. Recognise what you were. And that's why

they didn't really want you.'

David ducked as the blur flew towards him. The huge knife was thrown end-over-end with such velocity that it whistled through the air, the haft thumping into the wall-hanging behind him.

'I may just kill you next time. Then this ransom charade will end.'

David drew a breath and gathered his thoughts. 'You won't kill me.'

'Oh, no, what makes you think that? What makes you so certain?'

'Because then you'll have to relocate. Move this base. Find another place to operate from. Those in Mali who get the cut from your banditry will not be happy if you kill the golden goose.'

'Yes, this is a very convenient place, convenient for all of us. Of course, not so convenient for you,' and he laughed mirthlessly.

'Ahmed,' he shouted, 'remove this *kafir* from my sight. He is starting to bore me.'

David tried to think who the Sheikh reminded him of, with his mood swings and forced ill humour. Somehow a Qaddafi or Idi Amin came to mind. A person crossed between megalomania and schizophrenia.

The interlude in his room had given David material for thought. Something else to occupy his mind. He had seen what this man could do; the way poor Moussa was murdered.

The Sheikh had lost his code of honour, his *sharaf*. The deep and strict Bedouin morals of protecting the weak, as long as there was a strong man among men, and of hosting and entertaining, were missing.

And where Islam and the Koran places a high regard on the value of human life, this Sheikh did not.

The old traditions he had been born with, which would have

been rigorously enforced in childhood, were gone. He had been twisted and warped by his upbringing in some bizarre parallel way to others from his country.

Fifteen of the nineteen terrorists who had wreaked such damage and the loss of so many innocent lives on 11 September 2001 came from Saudi Arabia. Their upbringing and strict religious fundamentalism had twisted them, as well.

'So what the hell are you?'

It seemed as if David had taken on some form of amusement for him. Someone the Sheikh could chide and torment to fill an afternoon's spare hours. David thought that he was between missions as well. He wasn't just waiting for the *Marabout* to return with news of negotiations that would determine David's fate. There was an air about him, a restlessness; he was holding back for something else. A new illicit shipment, another hugely profitable high-risk smuggling venture.

'Come on South African, what are you doing in Mali?'

'I worked on a mine in the south west. Eighteen months ago my contract was completed.'

'But, pray tell me,' that sneering intonation, 'why are you still here? Why didn't you go back home?'

'I settled here.'

'What do you mean, settled here?'

David was reluctant to answer. Could there be some repercussion. Innocent people, Tecwwa, hurt elsewhere. Perhaps not, the Sheikh would never venture into an area more open and populated.

'I live in the Dogon country, at the bottom of the Bandiagara Escarpment.'

He looked sceptical. 'You live with the black monkeys. Are you yet another white man who has a black monkey woman?'

'No, my wife-to-be is a Tuareg lady.' *My God*, David thought, *I haven't even asked her yet!*

'Ah, the Tuareg. They are like the Bedouin but also not like the Bedouin.' He paused as if in contemplation. 'When the time came for us to fight, to unite, to win; we did it. When their time came to do the same, the Tuareg could not.'

'But at that time you had a strong leader. A man who was not only a warrior. Ibn-Saud also had stamina and bravery. But more than that he was a peace-maker. He treated the vanquished as equals. Ibn-Saud could bring peoples together. Smooth the differences.'

'You surprise me, South African, you are right in what you say!'

'But, he was also something more,' David went on.

'Pray tell me?' The sneer grated again.

'He was a true Sheikh!'

This time the Sheikh didn't miss, only it was a tea-glass that struck. Blood dripped from a cut high on David's forehead.

'Now, the Tuareg,' the Sheikh continued as if nothing had happened. 'My experience is that they have grown soft and lazy. Have lost their pride, become little shopkeepers and curio sellers. But they have more dignity and manners than the Berbers. And definitely more than my Maurs.'

David's bound hands grasped the hem of his t-shirt and wiped the blood that was dripping. 'Other than my wife-to-be I have only met a few. I agree with you though, they do seem to be losing their identity.'

The Sheikh nodded. 'There is a small Tuareg village not far from here, and don't get any ideas,' he said, pointing the *Khanja* dagger at David, 'they will not help you. Some time ago I conducted a little show for them, when I made this one of my bases.'

'I can imagine,' David murmured.

'No, you can't.'

The Sheikh leaned back a little and lit a cigarette. Almost effeminately he held it. 'You see those swords behind you?'

David looked around. 'Yes.'

'Why do you think I like to collect them? I have many others, of course.'

'I have a feeling that you prefer to use them, not just look at them.'

He smirked malevolently. 'The first pair are Nimcha,' drew on his cigarette, inhaled deeply, 'probably made in Morocco about three hundred years ago.'

The blades were menacingly sharp, yet elegant, with distinctly intricate hilts and handles.

'Next to them are Ida. Just big machetes, really. My pair once belonged to a Yoruba king who liked to separate his enemies, especially the leaders. Separate their heads from their bodies.'

He stood up and went over to the display. Taking one, he imitated a decapitation with an exaggerated swing, 'I have used it, too.'

In David's weakened and wasted state, the demonstration seemed pointless.

'The next pairs are amongst my favourites. The longer ones are called Flyssa, traditional swords of the Kabyles people.'

Artistically decorated with a brass inlay, the blades were fiercesomely long and heavy.

'You will appreciate the last two.'

'Why?'

His cold eyes glinted, 'Takoba swords. Made by .... guess who?'

David looked closely. There was something about them; the way in which the hilts and blades intersected. A close resemblance to a familiar jewellery design.

'The Tuareg?'

'I see that your mind still works, South African. Yes, they are Tuareg. I have tested them as well.'

'You have?'

'Oh yes, on the very same Tuareg in the village. The show I mentioned.'

'What did you do?'

He pointed one of the Takoba at David's heart. 'As a warning not to upset me, I reduced the already diminishing population by two!'

'Why did you choose this place,' David asked, 'for a base?'

'Hah, that is a very funny question.'

David noted that it did not make him laugh, though.

'The French Government told me about it. Where it was. In fact, I even moved a shipment for them through here.'

'Legitimately?'

'Are you taking the piss?'

'No, I'm just surprised by what you said.'

'The French have interests in Algeria. More important interests than peace.' He propped his head on one arm, as if in nonchalant contemplation.

'Like in Rwanda. Genocide followed.'

'Yes, that was hilarious. No, this was similar. But smaller, a more business-like operation.'

'And you've been here ever since.'

He shifted on his leather cushion, pulled another one closer to support his back.

'Somehow this location seems to suit my suppliers, and my customers, very well. Unfortunately, its suitability is probably lost on you.'

'You are wondering why I use this *Marabout*, this so-called holy man to do my negotiating. Why I don't do it myself?'

As each day passed now, David's ability to concentrate for even the slightest time was difficult. He found that he could barely speak, his tongue and voicebox rough and dehydrated.

'Maybe,' he said hoarsely, 'you are hiding behind him.'

The Sheikh's instantaneous rage was on him. With a shout he seized one of the Nimcha swords.

'I will kill you now.'

From outside the tent there was a stifled cough, as if someone was nervous about interrupting. One of his men came in. David couldn't make out what was being said, but the interlude was long enough to distract from the Sheikh's fury.

'What were we talking about? Oh, yes, the *Marabout*. I find their types very interesting.'

'Why?' David asked.

'They have this fervour which can either be genuine or put on. I like to watch when they go from one mode to the other.'

David struggled to get his thoughts in order. 'I'm not sure what they really are!'

The Sheikkh's sardonic face looked at him. '*Marabouts* used to be wandering priests, spreading Islam, spreading the Word of the Prophet. Respected and held in esteem. Respected not only by their converts, but also by those of other faiths and nationalities. They were treated like revered fathers.'

'What has changed?'

'They say the greed of the West is the cause.'

'The cause of what?'

'The cause of Jihad. The reason to conscientiously object, to promote active armed resistance.'

'Flying aeroplanes into buildings, killing thousands of innocents, including Muslims, is Jihad?'

What David thought might be a provocative question did not, in fact, phase the Sheikh. If anything, he seemed to want to talk about it.

'People living in the Arabic countries no longer want the will of the USA imposed on them. Men like Cheney and Bush and Rumsfeld, even Biden, so called leaders, are loathed by all. They are seen as invaders from a wasteful, self-serving society. And worse than that they are Semites, Jew lovers, propping up an arrogant and intolerant Israel. Israel is like a festering sore to all Arabs.'

'There is the other side of the coin too,' David muttered.

'What do you think is on the other side?' the Sheikh glared.

'There are Arab rulers who share almost nothing with their people. Rulers who have stashed the wealth of their countries into their own pockets.'

The Sheikh just looked at him, so he went on, 'Morocco, Algeria, Tunisia, Libya, Egypt, Jordan, Yemen, Syria, Sudan, there are so many.'

'You have forgotten the most important one,' the Sheikh stated coldly.

'No, I haven't. It is your own.'

Again the Sheikh seemed unruffled. In fact when he spoke next, his tone was disparaging. 'Saudi Arabia is the worst. Seven thousand so-called royal family members taking, stealing the spoils. Enjoying the wealth from the world's largest oil reserves. The wealth that really belongs to twenty eight million Saudis.'

'The time will come when the people will force change,' David said.

The Nimcha in the Sheikh's hand gleamed as he wiped it down with a cloth.

'Oh, yes, the time will come. As yours will too.'

Chapter 30
Imago

David was starting to feel very weak. And because he was so inactive, there was virtually no desire to eat. He had lost a lot of weight as well; his muscles too becoming thin and soft. Thirst seemed to be the only constant now; his tongue and throat so dry and sore, gums receding; teeth aching, a few felt loose. Ahmed gave him a mug of water four times a day. It was never enough.

Dreams and memories constantly overlapped. He could not really be sure which were which. Sometimes he simply slipped from daydreaming and dazed remembrance into sleep. Or he would awaken with a mirror-like recollection hovering behind his vision.

There had been a flash against the rocks and interwoven sand dunes. A fluid lighting – like movement that streaked horizontally off to his right and then was gone.

David brought his 4 x 4 to a halt, raised the binoculars to his eyes. Scanning the area he couldn't see anything, but there had been something. There it was, just the slightest tic; a momentary lifting of the tip of its tail, or maybe an ear that twitched.

So remarkably blending into its surroundings, the leopard lay on a low rock ledge observing him, its mottled black and brown coat perfectly camouflaged in the harsh Namibian landscape of the Hartmann's valley.

And even more unusual was the occurrence itself. This rare cat in the most remote location; not out of place, but very seldom heard of, almost never seen.

And. There had been that episode in Burkina Faso, near Oursi. It had been sadly amusing, an incident that David could not share with the two other Europeans who were there at the same time.

It must have happened more than a year and half ago now, just before he had met Tecwwa. He and Moussa had spent a month travelling in this largely unknown area; an unusual place of large shallow wetlands, surrounded by bare Sahelian dunes. Around the shores the local men caught mudfish and little boys trapped frogs and minnows; the washing which had been done by the village women weighted down by stones on the grassy banks.

The wonder lay in the wetlands themselves, thousands of birds; cormorants, geese, hamerkops, lapwings, godwits and so many more. Their calls and cries a blend of low and loud disharmony.

One night they had all sat around the dinner table in the camp run by the local Tuareg. David and Moussa, the headman, and two visiting European ornithologists accompanied by a conservation officer from Ouagadougou. The meal was served; strong-tasting pieces of fowl in a tomato and onion soup, with rice dished up separately.

The two ornithologists tucked in, the older, a Spanish man commenting on *how good the chicken tasted, real natural and free range!*

David didn't have the heart to tell him that what he was really eating were the duck that he had seen being plucked earlier that afternoon.

Garganey duck, the very migratory birds that they, the two experts, were studying and reporting on.

And. What was it about man and elephants? The relationships and esteem that can be forged and then shared with these impressive animals.

For so many centuries, millennia even, the desert elephants had circled from Mali into Burkina Faso and back. A route that took them from waterhole to waterhole, feeding area to feeding area. They led the nomads and shepherds to these distant and isolated places. The people recognised and respected this, in the driest of years it kept both them and their flocks alive.

A symbiotic tie ensuring both man and beast's survival.

David thought of his friend Cathan who had lived in Namibia for so many years. The desert elephants there had come to trust him implicitly. During their encounters they would bring their baby calves to meet him, with a tolerant pride that could not be concealed.

When his own son was tiny Cathan had returned the favour; the great females, interested and inquisitive, blowing breaths of warm slightly humid air over the little boy.

Their trunks gyrating in approval.

And. The weather-beaten blasting foreman who had worked for him for so many years. Every morning he would vigorously shake hands with all his colleagues and with those employed in his team; share a joke or tell a story. David believed he did this for a reason; a thought he kept to himself. The foreman prepared, handled and placed explosives and detonators. A careless mistake could easily lead to his demise; he was not prepared to die without having been courteous or, without being in a good mood.

David once asked him what he planned to do when he retired.

'Boss, I am going to take up bowls,' he told him.

'Take up bowls?'

'Yes, Boss.'

'Have you ever played before?'

'No, Boss. But that's not the reason why I'm going to start.'

The foreman had caught him; David knew he had to continue. 'Why are you going to, then?'

With an infectious, slightly lecherous laugh, the man replied. 'So that I can stand behind the ladies. You know, like when they bend down in their lovely white dresses to...' with a rounded flourish of his hands, he left the rest unsaid.

And. The extraordinary first impression made when, after the rains, tiny Mali girls would till the fields. They rode large camels which pulled ploughs, guided usually by their grandfathers.

The young, so young, maybe six or seven years old, working in unison with their elders and the farm animals.

And. Horses, brown. Horses, black. Horses, white. Horses, piebald. Horses, grey. Then one that looked different. A Takhi, a resemblance of the now extinct quagga, a wild tan-coloured horse with unique makings and stripes.

Flashbacks of a time spent in Mongolia. The nomadic farmer who would select a horse, ride it for a week. A different colour each time. An animal ridden to collapse, then probably never used again, returning to run with the herd.

A horse without a name. Merely a tool, a farm implement. For that week an isolated and never-named animal, receiving no sentiment or attachment.

The isolation and exhaustion of that horse was how David felt. But worse.

He was failing fast, succumbing to time.

And. The word just kept on circulating in David's head. Then found he was mumbling it; over and over.

'Atonement. Atonement. Atonement.'

Subconsciously he tried to connect it to something, tie his thoughts together.

Someone's face surfaced in his visions. A boy of about sixteen. A blond-haired lad standing on a dais; speaking, a eulogy, weeping as he looked down. Many mourners crying too.

Now David knew who he was; the son of a close friend. A friend who had ignored a sharp deep pain in the middle of a long and gruelling league squash match. Who, at the end of an attritional rally, had slumped to the floor, death almost instantaneous. His team mates and hapless opponent unable and powerless to save him.

But the anguish for atonement lay elsewhere.

The boy had argued with his Dad earlier that day, been rude, and then remaining sullen and morose.

A week later his father lay in the coffin in front of him; the boy's eyes pleading an apology.

It was, and would forever be, too late.

And. Would he ever see her again?

There seemed to be times when she felt so close. Moments sparked by something; the smell of tea, the fragrance of sage. In fits of reverie she appeared shimmering next to him. Somehow instilling strength, supporting his mind, his lizard mind; her voice in his ear. 'Please. Never to leave me. My David, please. You are my love.'

Chapter 31
Araouane

Tecwwa and Salim both saw it at the same time. From her lookout position on the bonnet, she raised her hand. Whitey immediately brought their slow-moving vehicle to a halt.

'What is it?' he asked, leaning out of the window.

Salim's deep voice replied, 'out to the right, in direction of one o'clock.'

Now it was clear to all of them, a fine plume of dust steadily drawing nearer.

'Quickly, Marie, Tecwwa, climb that dune,' Whitey pointed. 'Hide down below the crest. Tecwwa, take your rifle but keep it hidden. In your clothes. It mustn't reflect in the sunlight!'

Whitey grabbed his own weapon from the roof bracket. 'Come Salim, we must be close to the Araouane road. Let's see who's using it. Bring your machine gun. Keep it low!'

From behind a low outcrop of boulders, the two men watched the vehicle barrelling down the corrugated road towards them.

'They're driving too fast, will never see us,' Whitey murmured.

Through his binoculars he could see two men in the driver's cab. There appeared to be a third person sitting in the loading box at the back.

'Salim, see what you can make out.' Whitey handed the binoculars over to the giant.

Salim studied the vehicle intently until it was past. They continued to watch as it bore on in the direction of Tombouctou.

'It is government car from military. I think military man driving.'

Whitey agreed. 'Who else did you see?'

'There were two more men.' Salim appeared to be puzzled.

'Tuaregs?'

'No, Whitey, clothes wrong colour. Like not usual. I think they are Muslims. Like priest. Maybe senior, like Imam.'

'More like *Marabout*,' the white man muttered bleakly.

With the sound of the vehicle fading away and the dust settling down, Whitey and Salim made their way back to their own car.

Whitey called out, and the two women slid down the dune to join them.

'Did they see us?' Marie asked worriedly.

'No, not at all. But we'll stay here until it gets dark.'

Marie fetched her notebook and maps. Whilst Tecwwa made tea over a small primus stove, Whitey plotted their position, talking them through the planning for the coming days.

'We are here.' He pointed to the map with his pencil and paused; '.... still about sixty kilometres from Araouane. Staying on the old North-South track will take us another seven or eight hours. At best. We have only being doing about ten kilometres per hour. But if we use the road, it will be a lot quicker.'

The others listened closely; for they suspected, almost knew that Whitey would have a surprise for them.

'We need to be in Araouane first thing tomorrow.'

Tecwwa looked surprised; this was sooner than she imagined.

'But?' Marie asked.

'You will go there without me.'

'Whitey, we can't do that!' Marie exclaimed. 'It's too dangerous.'

Whitey looked around, scrutinised each of them in turn. His fierce eyes saw the concern in theirs, even Salim was perturbed.

'This is how I see it. I have a feeling that the vehicle which passed us earlier was on a mission. Either carrying a message to, or from someone. And I suspect it will be returning.'

'How can you be sure?' Tecwwa asked.

'Look at where we are. Look at the scenery. Look at the sky. Look to the horizon. Look all around you. What do you see?'

They were perplexed.

'Nothing,' said Tecwwa hesitantly.

'Precisely. There is nothing. Except for the small village, Araouane, up the road and a solitary car that races past. There is also something else about that car.'

'Something about the people in it?' Salim sonorous voice enquired.

'No. It's about the people not in it.'

'Whitey, you are talking in riddles,' Marie frowned.

'No, I'm not. Work it out.'

Tecwwa nodded her head. 'In remote place like this, car would be full. Too full, on top, back, even on roof. With village people looking for lift, maybe to go doctor in Tombouctou. Maybe with women who go market. Maybe even animals loaded, goats and chickens for market. Big drums for water or gasoline.'

'Exactly,' the white man went on. 'It would be overloaded, not virtually empty.'

Tecwwa poured more tea for them all. Then Whitey continued. 'What we do not know is if, or when, it's coming back.'

'But why is that important? Maybe they'll just use a telephone.' Marie's brow was furrowed as she tried to establish the train of Whitey's thinking.

'No, *cariad*,' Whitey replied, keeping his voice calm and considerate. 'Nothing operates out here, there is no infrastructure, no networks or anything. The only possibility would be a satellite telephone, and somehow I don't think that's an option. Calls are too easily tracked down.'

'You are right,' Marie sipped her tea. 'What else?'

'Now remember,' he said, 'we need to get some assistance. Recruit a few men to help us.'

'Yes, yes, I will find,' Tecwwa cut in firmly.

'Well, if that car does return and I think it will within a day or two. And if it stops in Araouane while we are all there ....' he paused again.

The two women looked ill at ease.

'That is why I can't go with you. I have to be the backup support.'

'You want us to capture them?' Salim asked.

'No, no. If David is still alive out here in this godforsaken place, and if those messengers don't return to where he is, he will die. A sign that anything is not as it should be, will surely mean the end for him.'

Tecwwa's lips started to tremble but she held herself together.

'What we are going to do is this. The three of you will go into Araouane tomorrow. Before you get there I will leave you. On foot. About ten kilometres out.'

Marie took his hand. 'And then?'

'I'll hike around. Find a vantage point just north of the village. If that vehicle doesn't stop, give it two hours and then follow on out in the same direction. I'll meet you on the track.'

'And, Whitey, if it does stop?' Tecwwa was still close to tears.

'Then you must detain them immediately. Don't let them get away. I'll be watching. Don't worry, I'll come and help you.'

His countenance was stern and implacable. 'And, if by some chance they have a satellite telephone, make sure it is switched off. Salim, if necessary you must destroy it.'

Araouane was drowning under the invading sand.

Half-lying on an old wicker couch across from Tecwwa, Marie and Salim, the old leader's voice was sad as he spoke of the village's legacy.

'In my past fathers' times, three-four hundred years ago, this was important place. For worship, for Islamic study, for learning of culture. Holy men came from far, from Egypt, from Maroc, from many, many places. In recent times some white people have even come here. They say to help us. They left too.'

He sighed. 'When I am dead, so too will Araouane die. We are unable to stop the destiny.'

His face was completely covered by a light blue, slightly grimy headscarf. Only his rheumy eyes were unconcealed.

Marie thought that he was probably losing his sight. Certainly the old man had difficulty in focusing on them properly.

Not surprisingly, their arrival had caused some animation, if a little restrained. A few women hovered around; one had come forward and after listening to Tecwwa had led them to a small, slightly run-down house in the centre of the village.

The community appeared to be almost totally female, the children small, and most looked malnourished. Carefully Tecwwa greeted everybody, the few people there had responded quietly. Even Marie could detect the polite deference in their replies.

Tecwwa explained. 'They know by the way I speak that I am born from Ihaggaren. From noble family. They see too that we have motor vehicle and body guard. To them, we must have great wealth.'

'You say that you are from Adrar des Ifôghas.' The old Tuareg peered in their direction. Some of the village women had joined him to listen to the conversation. Life for them was so sedentary and mundane; now there was a diversion, something of interest happening.

'Yes, I was born there. But for many years I have lived in the

Bandiagara Falaise.'

'And the people with you?'

'They are from the west, from Bamako way.'

'That is very far. You are all very far from home. And you have no military escort. That is very unusual. Very dangerous. You should not be here,' he said sternly.

Tecwwa knew that she had to explain and keep the discussion going. Trust needed to be built.

Before she could speak, however, the old man carried on. 'You say you are originally from Ifôghas?'

'Yes, I am from that place,' she repeated.

'And your name again?'

'Tecwwa. My heritage name is Ag Heguir.'

Abruptly the old Tuareg's attention changed. 'You are family of Khyar ag Heguir?'

'Yes, he was my grandfather's brother. He was a man of many years when my father was born.'

His whole demeanour transformed as the realisation struck. He sat upright. This was a member of one of the most respected names in Tuareg hierarchy, sitting in front of him. A name that recalled peace and justice and wisdom from his childhood, from an era of his own parents and grandparents.

'Bring *eghale*, bring tea and water,' he gestured. 'These are important guests.'

Two of the local women scurried away.

When the women returned with the refreshments, more people accompanied them, crowding into the room.

With a quiet word to Tecwwa and Marie, Salim left, went to stand outside near the vehicle. From there he could observe the access routes to Araouane, and be close to their weapons.

He knew that Tecwwa and Marie were in no present danger. If anything, Tecwwa was in control of the situation.

'Why are you here then?' the old Tuareg asked. Tea had been served in small shot glasses.

'I have come to look for my husband,' Tecwwa said firmly.

'Your husband cannot be in Araouane. There are only six men here including myself. And two of them have dying disease.'

Tecwwa was about to speak, but he continued talking. 'Our other men, including my grandsons, work far away. In Taoudenni. In the salt mines. Your husband cannot be there either. We are not of your class.'

'You are right, Father.' Tecwwa looked at Marie, translated what had been said.

Then she spoke proudly and clearly with that dark light of passion in her eyes. 'My husband is not Tuareg. He is a white man, an English speaking man.'

The gasp was simultaneous and audible from the assembled group. Some of the women pulled their face veils up high to conceal their expressions. They drew closer together as if to ward off evil, shield themselves from something malevolent.

'Sheikh Saffah,' one of them moaned. 'Sheikh Saffah!'

Tecwwa and Marie looked at each other, confused by the words. The reaction from the group did not really surprise them. They knew that their presence had already created a subdued consternation. But the fear and anxiety that now arose so rapidly was another matter altogether. Vividly the peril, the insecurity they faced, was brought home.

The old man's response would be important.

'You... you should leave this place,' he said quietly, his voice grim. 'Right away!'

Tecwwa could, however, sense that he was struggling with the situation. His respect for her name and status, his role as host and elder, sat deep within his being; rooted in the foundations of his moral code and Tuareg upbringing.

She knew what to say next. It could not be refused.

'Father, I am asking for your help.'

Silence seemed to stretch.

Slowly the old Tuareg stood up; shakily he shuffled across the room. 'Follow me.'

One of the women joined them, taking his arm to support him. Painstakingly they made their way down a dust and dirt-strewn alleyway to the eastern edge of the old town, to the very last house, with the desert expanse spreading out in front of them.

Ducking through a low doorway, they entered a small dim antechamber. The smell was appalling; of excrement and blood, sweat and urine. The room itself was clean; the odour came from a thin foam mattress and the man lying on it.

What remained of a man.

As their eyes grew accustomed to the light, Tecwwa and Marie could see the mutilation. Legs without feet, arms without hands, sockets without eyes.

Marie turned, her stomach heaving, rushed out and was violently sick, vomit spewing, almost before she could hunch down in the sand.

Tecwwa remained behind, taking in the gruesome yet still-living sight.

'This is my first-born son. My second son did not survive,' the old man said gruffly.

'How did....?' Tecwwa could not complete the question.

'I do not know why he lived. Maybe the shock slowed his blood. Maybe his life spirit was too strong. Maybe we fixed the tourniquets just in time.'

'Who did this? And why?'

'The why was to intimidate us into submission. To force us into silence.'

He drew a deep breath. 'The who... is Sheikh Saffah. The Butcher.'

'And?'

'Your English man is in his hands. In the hands of the Butcher.'

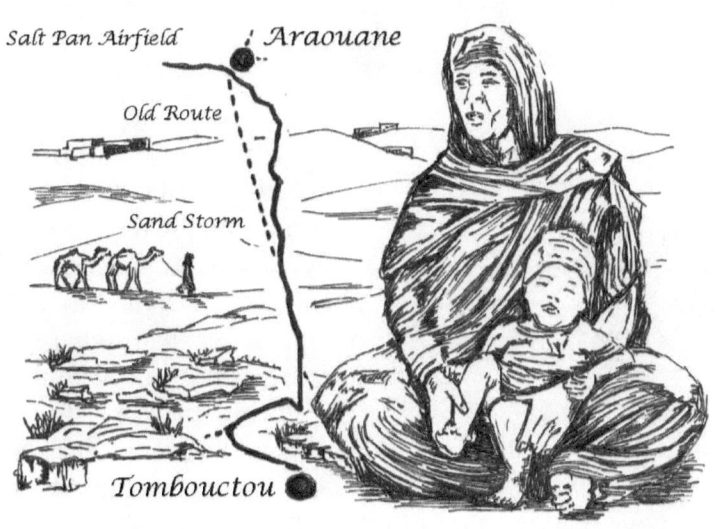

Salt Pan Airfield

Araouane

Old Route

Sand Storm

Tombouctou

Chapter 32
Tachelt

From within his dugout, Whitey watched the village, a settlement declining by the day.

As usual for such a remote place, the arrival of his three companions had caused some interest. But even from a distance the local people still looked listless and poverty-stricken.

He caught a glimpse of Marie and Tecwwa walking through the village; later saw Salim take up a position in the shade near their car.

In the afternoon, a few of the women went to fetch water from a well. Another slowly herded a flock of goats together, bringing them in to a *kraal* nearby. Late in the day two Tuareg men arrived, a line of fifteen camels behind them. The camels were unladen, probably going to, or coming from some far-away market.

There was the last moment of daylight; night fell, and a still-deep darkness took over.

Whitey lay there unmoving, awake and observant.

The next day, just after noon and where nothing had passed for three days, Whitey heard a vehicle.

Salim had heard it too.

The big man took up a position behind a low broken-down wall, his sub-machine gun at the ready. There was a split moment when Whitey saw Tecwwa crouching below a window-opening facing the rutted road. Of Marie, there was no sign.

For a while there seemed to be a period of hiatus, a concealed breathless expectancy. A smoke-like suspense.

But the vehicle went by without stopping.

It was as before; the same vehicle, three people in it, otherwise just as empty.

The village Elder knew that he was compelled to help. Their Tuareg lifestyle had changed so much, but honour was bound to duty, and to him, both were sacrosanct.

And more than that, there was revenge to be exacted. There was retribution to be taken for what had been done to him and his sons. Tuareg women had, through history, fought at the sides or in defence of their men. Now there was one sitting before him who would be the same: fearless, determined and, if necessary, vicious.

The Elder looked at her unveiled face and for a moment marvelled at her beauty. He could see the steel in her eyes; they seemed to replicate the blade that killed one son and so terribly mutilated another.

The white man in captivity and my fellow Tuareg woman must be united in something special. It was a thought he did not utter aloud.

As they sat there, the men of the village slowly joined in. With the two recently-arrived camel herders, there were now nine in all. Even the two afflicted by Aids were present. One of them was so weak, he could barely walk or even talk.

'We need to remove this bandit from our area. This Sheikh Safah who has damaged our community, taken our land. We cannot go near there anymore. To find grazing for our goats and camels.' The elder was trying to muster an aggression and determination that his advanced years no longer allowed.

'We have not been near that place since before him. Since from the time when the French legionnaires were there.' The speaker's robe and veil were dirty and bedraggled, his voice rough and dissenting. 'Before I was even born.'

'Yes, I know. But my sons need to be avenged.'

The dissenter spoke again.

'What can we do against a military man who has soldiers and weapons? Who knows how to attack and more importantly knows how to defend? What can we do with two women, one soft and European; and an ape mountain,' he sneered, careful not to include or insult Tecwwa to her face.

When Tecwwa spoke, her voice was cold and low and penetrating. 'In the past we would not have allowed an intruder to take something away from us. And now, when we, as Tuareg, have already lost so much, our way of life, our freedom to travel, to trade; our freedom curtailed by lines drawn on maps, by people who knew little of our ways. Where foreign people have created the misery and poverty in this village; I think it is time to remove this foreign intruder.'

'You are only saying this because you want your rich white man back;' This time, the barb was not held back.

Marie struggled to comprehend what was going on. The words had no meaning; there was not a single one she understood. Unlike the Tuareg women, the men kept their faces fully veiled: she could not judge expression or visual demeanour.

But she felt Tecwwa's anger.

Some of the men saw it in Tecwwa's face too; the deflagrating fire of will and concealed fury.

But Tecwwa remained ice-calm and resolute. She looked around and then continued. 'Everyone here knows the situation. We are going to try and rescue my husband. If possible, we need three men to help us.'

'You have a plan?' one of the men asked.

Tecwwa paused before replying, for she had no real answer. Whitey was not there. She was not prepared to either compromise him, or even let the gathering know that he was nearby.

'We have a plan, it will be revealed when we leave. When we are ready.'

'Will we be paid?' the uncouth individual queried.

The old village chieftain started to talk about tribal obligations, protection of their own, but Tecwwa quietly intervened.

'I will pay.'

Whitey waited. He didn't feel tired, it was time to begin the pursuit.

Salim was checking their Land Cruiser. Whitey watched as the bonnet was opened, then the tyres were checked. What looked like bedding rolls were placed in the back.

'Nobody will be using those, of that I am sure,' he said to himself. 'Tecwwa must have found extra men, though.'

Two hours passed before he moved. Slipping out of the dugout, he made his way down to the track that led northwards. In the early afternoon it was scorching, a blanketing oppressive heat of 45°C.

When they arrived, Whitey was waiting for them at the side of the road. Marie was driving slowly, Tecwwa next to her in the front. Salim stood at the back with his machine gun ready. Three other men sat in the loading box.

I don't think my big friend trusts them very much, Whitey reflected wryly.

When Marie pulled up, he could see the relief in her face. She was about to start crying. The shock of the terribly maimed and disfigured man welled up within her; she needed to tell Whitey about it but realised this was not the time. With a deep breath she composed herself, just held his hand briefly.

'*Aros yn gryf, fy anwyl.* Be strong, my darling,' Whitey responded.

There was a flurry of animated chatter from the accompanying Tuareg. One in particular seemed to be more raucous and argumentative than the others.

Whitey asked Tecwwa to translate.

'They want to know who you are?'

'Why?'

'The one, Hosseyni, he says he has seen your kind before.'

Whitey's fierce, sharp eyes examined the grubby-robed man in question.

'What kind am I?' he said coolly.

'He says you are…' Tecwwa struggled with the English word, 'soldier for money … mercenarist? They now want more money to help us.'

'Tell him, I am no mercenary. There is to be no additional payment. If he wants, they can all return to the village.' Whitey paused, '…and they have one minute to decide.'

In that brief interlude, Whitey had already worked Hosseyni out. He would talk to Salim about it later.

After conferring with her Tuareg recruits, Tecwwa spoke to Whitey. 'We are about twelve kilometres away.'

'Time for us to get off the track and move into the desert. Set up camp,' he replied.

He called to Salim. 'Take Bahedi with you, follow us on foot. Use the spade and broom, cover over our spoor. I will stop when we are hidden away from the track.'

Five kilometres north of Araoaune they had swung left, heading westerly towards Mauritania. Occasionally they saw fresh tyre-outlines of the car in front of them.

The journey had been difficult: slow grinding through the thick-grained clutching sand, and with tyres deflated. But there were unexpected benefits. With their progress so slow there was virtually no dust. And they were driving into a slight headwind, which carried the low throbbing engine noise back away from them.

If conditions had been any different, Whitey would have stopped earlier.

'Tecwwa, tell me about these men.'

In her eyes he could still see the iron determination, but

outwardly she appeared concerned and worried. The stress was getting to her; the knowledge that they were getting closer to David's captors, the uncertainty of whether David was still alive. The foreboding that he may already be dead.

'One we can trust. Village chief say he is like brother, a brother in blood to the dead son.'

'That is Bahedi?'

'Yes, Bahedi. Other man Nagim. Also okay. I think he not too clever. With brain. Maybe only good for observing. Tell us what he see.'

'And Hosseyni?'

'He with big mouth... I not sure.'

Whitey nodded, 'I cannot see their faces. But I agree with you.' He said no more. Salim had already been briefed, knew what to do.

While the two women prepared food for the men to eat, quietly and thoroughly Whitey outlined his plans.

'We leave just before midnight. This should give us five hours to get into position.'

He stopped to allow Tecwwa to translate.

'We will each remain in a fixed position. Each of us will have an observation point. You do not move from where I place you.'

Carefully, Tecwwa conveyed his instructions.

'If you have to, you piss where you lie.'

There was a knowing cough of agreement from Bahedi.

'I will come to each of you when the time is right. Will show you what to do next.'

One of the men said something.

'This man wants to know how long they must wait. He also asks about guns for them?'

Whitey answered the first question, ignored the second one. 'The vehicle in front of us with three men in it? The vehicle we are following. We want it to convey its message. We take no action until it leaves.'

'Why?'

This time it was Tecwwa questioning.

'If their message is successful, maybe David will be with them. Then our target changes.'

'And if not?'

'We will then go in to find him.'

Whitey looked at Marie. He could sense her state of worry, see the trepidation in her face.

'Tecwwa, you and Marie must wait for us here. Guard our vehicle. It will be our lifeline.'

Tecwwa looked dejected, but Whitey was adamant.

'You have to be ready. Ready to treat David if we get him out.'

By the time dawn broke, Whitey had his men in place.

On foot they had made their way through the low dunes, with Bahedi leading until they were within sight of the airfield. Some four hundred metres was close enough. Whitey wanted to be able to observe clearly, yet still have suffcient distance between the bandits and his small team. An animal could easily be disturbed or a dog set barking.

And then there were the three men that Tecwwa had recruited in Araouane. Could he and Salim really trust them? Whitey was sure Hosseyni would renege, might in some way try and warn the Sheikh. Probably for monetary gain only. Whitey's inner view was that the Sheikh would probably kill an informant, not reward one.

However the situation developed, the secrecy and concealment of his men was paramount. Carefully he positioned the three Tuareg recuits, each on an axis point of the compass; east, north and west. Salim covered the track which led south before it changed direction back eastwards to Araouane.

Whitey kept in no fixed position. Continually he moved around from point to point, spending time with each man; with hand gestures and sign language indicating caution and stillness.

More importantly, if one of the Tuaregs did break for it and give the game away, Whitey wanted to be nearby and flexible to deal with any situation. He was sure Hosseyni would turn traitor. There was a sly and devious greed to the man. Without Hosseyni knowing it, Salim's silenced rifle was always trained on him.

Making use of a piece of khaki-coloured cloth to screen his binoculars from reflecting in the early morning sunlight, Whitey studied the camp. There was a sturdy structure built of canvas, shade netting and poles. It was surrounded on three sides by a high wooden fence, clearly erected to form a screen against the prevailing winds and continually moving sand. Alongside were more tents, single-man military issue, pitched around an open fire pit. In front of each of the small tents, a figure lay sleeping.

Whitey counted them off. *One, two, three, four. Probably the three visitors in the big tent. With the main man.*

Further off, and out in the open closer to the dunes, was a small blue shelter with a flimsy translucent roof.

To one side of the landing strip and next to an overhead tank and handpump, rows of oil drums were stacked. At the end of the airfield, a torn and tattered windsock hung motionless in the still air.

The government vehicle was still there, parked next to two others. Intently Whitey studied them.

'David's Land Rover,' he breathed. 'I'm sure of it. The roof rack is the one we made together.'

Whitey and his men watched and waited; saw the awakening of a desert camp. A man stoked the fire into flames. Others crept out from their bedding rolls to urinate, squatting thirty metres from where they had slept. One walked over to the blue shelter. He appeared to have something in his hand.

Looks like a mug. Water, Whitey thought. *Somebody must be in there.*

But one thing was blatantly obvious. Discipline had become slack. To Whitey's trained eyes it was clear that the bandit group thought that there was no danger, no threat from anyone. *They have no sentries, not even a casual patrol or walk-around.*

The enemy had become careless and lax. A sandbagged dugout on a small hill adjacent to the airfield was clearly unmanned and unprotected.

Just as Whitey spoke, one of those lounging around got up and went to it and disappeared from view. A few minutes the man emerged, adjusting his robe.

'Probably went for a shit,' Whitey whispered. 'They believe they cannot be touched. I wonder why that is? Why do they think they are so safe?'

Whitey lay just below the crest of a small dune, mulling over his own question, pondering over answers as his eyes took in the bandits' camp.

The comparison he formed was to the piracy in Somalia. In his head, he built the case.

They smuggle and kidnap to raise cash. Where smuggling used to be a way of life, they now reason it to be legitimate.

Unscrupulous armaments companies and their surrogate salesmen, the arms dealers, instigate and fuel wars in their own selfish interest.

Smugglers and pirates are part of the shipping chain.

And kidnapping has become part of the deal too. European governments and wealthy families will pay the ransoms in the misguided belief that some of the money will find its way to the local populace. Throw money at the problem, rather than getting their hands dirty and trying to help repair a broken and decrepit economy; trying to help people crushed by violence and plunder. Continuing to allow education to remain stifled. Then recognising leaders who emerge. Leaders who are often as bad as the raping perpetrators already in place.

'The same here; in this case,' Whitey said to himself, 'somebody has seen a gap and is taking the money. For themselves only, for no-one else.'

Twice that morning he carefully crawled around to his men, reassuring each one with a firm touch on the shoulder.

Whitey touched them on purpose. Bahedi and Nagim seemed to be relaxed, almost sleepy. He cautioned them into vigilance.

In Hosseyni though, he could detect an anxious tension.

Whitey moved across to Salim. 'Watch Hosseyni like a hawk. If he moves towards that camp, stop him. Dead!'

Just before midday, three men emerged from the main shelter. Two were dressed in flowing Islamic robes, the third in a Malian army uniform.

There were no farewell gestures or handshakes. The military man started his vehicle and within a minute they had departed, driving down the airstrip and off into the distance: dust raising as their speed increased.

Almost at the same time, a man stood up and headed towards the blue shelter. Again, there was something in his hand.

It was a scene in torpor; airless, windless and fearsomely hot. All the bandits lay in the shade of their tents.

Security was non-existent.

Whitey scrutinised the camp and then his men; his binoculars sweeping slowly across the terrain.

He could see that Salim was alert, had his arm raised, pointing.

Bahedi and Nagim were in their places. Hosseyni was not.

Then Whitey had him in his sights.

Hosseyni was about two hundred and fifty metres away, creeping low and closer towards the bandits' camp.

His eye killing, cold through the rifle-scope, Whitey didn't even hesitate; neither did Salim.

The two silenced shots were virtually simultaneous.

Blood seeping through his headdress, the Tuareg lay face down, inert in the desert, concealed by a bank of sand. Whitey had told him not to move from his position, shown him not to move from his position; now he would never move again.

In the main tent the Sheikh stirred, pushed his water pipe away.

He sensed a disturbance, what it was he did not know.

Some slight unusual sound. A sharp faint crack; like a dry twig being snapped.

He got up and walked to the entrance, stood there and looked out into the blinding sunlight. For a long time he was motionless, his eyes searching.

But there was nothing unusual or untoward that he could detect.

His men were all resting, their few animals equally somnolent in the heat.

What he could not see, however, were the four pairs of eyes watching him.

'I need the toilet,' Marie said to Tecwwa. 'I'll go behind that hill over there,' she pointed.

'Be careful, take my gun,' Tecwwa murmured.

'No, I won't need it, will only be gone for a few minutes.'

The sun was going down and in the moat where she squatted, the intense heat starting to wane.

It was only when her eyesight was near to ground level that she saw the sand mounds; the s-shaped tracks. Worriedly, she looked around.

'My God, they are everywhere.'

Marie was overcome and frozen in position by a dread, the like of which she had never known before.

Behind her back there was an eerie slithering whisper that got closer and closer. In front of her she could see movement too; her intrusion had agitated them.

Slowly, terror stricken, Marie swivelled her head from side to side, trying to find an avenue of escape.

She tried to call out. But her throat choked shut. No sound could, or would emerge.

Down between her spread feet one emerged; its triangular horned head moving on until half of its body became visible.

Marie was petrified, her heart seemed to be arresting. The deepest and coldest of fears overwhelming her.

She was surrounded by snakes, hordes of horned vipers, all of which were attuned to her and her fear.

Marie could feel her mind going. The frozen horror melting into panic.

The closest snake, the one that passed right beneath her, had turned around. Pitch-dark eyes with pupils vertical speared her soul. Its body tense; if Marie moved, even slightly, she believed the snake would attack. All the others had stopped moving, seemed to be settling down, as if no longer concerned or disturbed.

Out of nowhere and from deep within her, through the mind-shaking fear, Whitey's voice reverberated. *Sometimes you have to take a bullet, to save taking another. You might survive one, but more than that, the odds of survival become exponentially less.*

Marie started to calm now that she had heard him. Their years together; Whitey's enormous mental strength, his will of steel, slowly brought courage seeping back into her.

She could see that slightly to her left there appeared to be fewer of them. For some unapparent reason it was as if a slight path had opened up.

As always in the desert, the last light was fading fast. Through her diminishing panic, Marie knew that she only had a few minutes left: maybe ten or fifteen at the outside.

Carefully she stabilised herself and drew a deep breath. Prepared to stand.

'If I take the bite,' she whimpered inwardly, 'the right side, away from the heart. Away from my legs. That is all I know.'

With a lurch, her legs slightly buckling from being bent so long, she stood. It was the lurch that made her later life easier.

The horned viper, when it stuck, hit her trailing right hand. She would later lose it to above the wrist.

Born left-handed, fortune had favoured her.

Out where the men were, darkness had fallen too. It was after eight o'clock, there was no moon. The only glimmer of light came from the bandits' campfire.

Whitey had brought his men together. He spoke to Salim.

'I need to see inside that blue shelter,' he whispered. 'See who, or what, is inside there.'

Salim nodded, but didn't say anything. Bahedi and Nagim didn't say anything either. Any doubts they may have had in attempting a rescue were removed. Their obedience now bluntly reinforced by the killing of Hosseyni.

'Wait for me here. If I don't return before midnight, leave. Go back to the women. Straight away. Then get out of this place. Fast!'

Again Salim nodded, his eyes expressively wide.

Melting away into the darkness, Whitey was gone.

He had already planned the route in the daylight; his movements now quick and assured.

A rocky patch was circumvented. The sound of a rock clattering would be like a thunderclap. He kept well away from the reflective fire. Around it, he could hear the bandits talking. There were some guttural words and cross-talk, followed by harsh, raucous laughter.

There were other sounds that were difficult to make out. Whitey lay there, listening intently. Then he knew what they were; it was a sound familiar to him from his past.

Knives were being sharpened.

As silent as a wraith, he moved on until he was tight up against the blue netting.

Whitey looked around carefully.

The bandits had stoked the fire. Silhouetted in the increased light, one of them was moving towards him.

Ever so slowly, Whitey removed a garrotte from his pocket. Like a marauding leopard, covert in a thicket, he lay tensed and ready to pounce.

Then the danger passed.

The bandit flicked on a torch and opened a flap in the netting. There was a tin mug in his hand. With some care he lifted the lying man's head and turned the man's face towards him.

For a split second, and despite the blindfold, David was clearly visible; his gaunt, sun-hurt face distinct in the torchlight.

Chapter 33
Rescue

He was seldom lucid now.

At first it had been slow, but now he knew that his body was shutting down. His life spirit was flickering. In another day or two he would die. Probably go; unconscious then dead. Or they would just kill him.

The man designated to look after him, Ahmed, his guard, had to support him when he urinated or defecated. Even then his waste was so little, urine a dark blood - coloured yellow, faeces like dried rabbit pellets.

He had been held captive for so long; time, days, months, had become meaningless. There was nothing to be desired; no hunger, no thirst. His quest for freedom had virtually faded away, was now almost dormant.

A white man incarcerated in the harshest of environments, deep in the Sahara. His capture by Islamic bandits.

All this had doomed him.

He knew it.

Everything was startlingly clear in the brief moments when he was alert. Remembrance of long forgotten incidents from his youth, dates of meetings and events going back years, surnames of people whom he may have met only once, old sporting results.

He listened as the negotiator, the Marabout, spoke to his captors for the last time.

'There is no money, no agreement. His government refuses to pay.'

'The infidel will be slaughtered.'

The Arabic words were difficult to follow, but he knew

enough to understand.

Through the blindfold he could sense Ahmed's eyes turned towards him. Was there a compassion, a feeling of sympathy, or merely an acknowledgement that his fate had been determined?

It was late and very quiet. The men asleep in their blankets around the ebbing fire. The intense desert cold had brought him out of delirium. Or was it something else? A sound, like a muted gurgle, a faint noise out of place. There was a light touch on his shoulder, a whisper where the blindfold crossed his ear.

'*Brawd bach*, keep very quiet, keep the faith; *ons het jou kom haal.*'

'Come to fetch me?' Was he dreaming, hallucinating, wishing words into his head? Imagining release yet again.

Yet there was only one man that would mix Welsh, English and South African Afrikaans in a single sentence and in the knowledge that he would understand.

Whitey le Roux; here?

He felt himself being lifted, drawn up across a wide set of shoulders. There was a steadying moment as the man carrying him got the weight right. A broad balancing stride and they were off into the desert.

After what seemed to be an hour to him, but in fact it took much longer, the big man lowered him gently to the ground.

A trickle of water passed over his lips, the blindfold removed. A knife cut the ropes binding his hands and legs.

'We would have done this earlier, but it was easier to carry you still tied up.'

He looked around. It was getting lighter as dawn began to break.

Whitey was kneeling with a water bottle. Three other men stood around. Two of them were dressed in long flowing royal-blue robes and wrap-around face veils that only the Tuareg men wear; the third, the man who had carried him, a black giant with a large white toothed smile.

And then they all moved aside.

She looked, and then was down beside him. Her soft clear voice shook as she spoke.

'My dear one, you are still alive. We will never be separated again. My world is behind me.'

Chapter 34
Retribution

 Whitey only spoke of it once; at the hospital where Marie was due for release the next day. She was happy and rested and strong; her pregnancy blooming, not affected by the trauma of an amputation.

The suffering that David had gone through and would still; he was so ill and damaged; the shock that Marie had endured and now come through, Whitey felt that they should at least know that the job had been done properly.

'Salim and I took the four bandits by the fire very quickly. It was over in minutes.'

The brutality of the killings he kept to himself.

Stealthily silent and methodically dispassionate, they had taken them out. One by one. Salim's bare hands had snapped the necks of two; Whitey had used a garrotte.

The last bandit stirred awake as Whitey drew the wire across his throat. There was a voiceless spume as the dying man's throat spurted blood-froth and mucus.

'And the Sheikh Butcher?' Tecwwa asked.

Whitey paused before answering.

'We caught him at the back. He must have heard something. Was trying to slip out into the desert.'

'And?'

The Butcher did not look around before raising his revolver to shoot Whitey; did not see Salim, could not evade the short vicious blow that clubbed him down.

'What happened next?'

'The two Tuareg with us, they found these swords. Ones that

had been on display.'

'Nimcha, Ida, Flyssa, Takoba,' David muttered.

Whitey could not tell them of the all-too-quick subsequent dismemberment of the man. At the end, with a wide clean swing of the Takoba, the Tuareg Nagim beheaded him.

The head of Sheikh Safah the Butcher, consigned to the dirt, to be removed and eaten by jackals.

Siné-Saloum Delta

Senegal

Seven years on ....

Between them, it had taken more than two years to nurse David back to health and full fitness. Her brother's life saved by the donation and transplant of one of her kidneys.

She loved this place, had never been happier than now, living with her brother and his beautiful Tuareg wife. The move from Australia was easier than expected. She taught at the little school in a nearby fishing village. A small speed boat was her mode of transport to work.

Tecwwa had helped her heal, too. The demons and fears she had harboured since childhood had all but disappeared.

Through the kitchen window, where she was preparing the evening meal, for it was her turn that night, she watched the two of them as they sat out on the deck together. David and Tecwwa were holding hands and talking quietly, watching the African darters straggling in, finding their roosting perches high up in the baobab tree forest.

From far off came the last call of a fish eagle, its evening cry ringing and evocative.

In front of them the wide river was somnolent down into the delta. The hue on the water changed colour as the sun sank, from blue to brown, through pinks and umber-oranges. Quickly the sky became night, and the river black.

Every day she paused to wonder at how life was here. Sometimes the villagers would arrive by canoe. Her sister-in-law would considerately treat and medicate them with a knowledge garnered over so many years. The bush telegraph was an amazing phenomenon. They had only just settled here when, shortly thereafter, the first local woman appeared seeking help.

For a moment her mind clouded as she remembered poor Tana, poor joyful Tana who met the wrong man after the death of Moussa. Her grave was always carefully tended.

Once a year they all went to Dakar, where her brother supervised any renovations and repairs that needed to be done to a proud matriarch's home. The woman living there never had to pay anything; this had already been dealt with. The matriarch understood that there was a deep debt to be repaid. Within her very limited means she responded, and made up little thank-you gifts. Promises were exacted that these were only to be opened when her visitors return to their delta island home.

And the joys of the children. The elaborate organisation that took place when they all visited. There were now five of them. All had Tuareg middle names, Erza and Akali; Hadia, Lala and Anta;

for Tecwwa was their doting godmother. Two solemn little boys who loved wrestling and football, wrestling in particular. Their father was a heavyweight champion, after all.

And where for years Whitey couldn't face a child without shame in his heart, there were now three excitable and exuberant girls. Three girls who had been taught by their proud and soft-hearted father to sing so wonderfully.

Celtic songs of praise, folk songs in Welsh; French and Italian operatic arias and serenades.

Lovely as an angel
come down on earth
fresh as the lily
that opens at dawn;
eyes that speak and laugh,
a look that wins the heart,
hair darker than ebony,
an enchanting smile.

TRANSLATIONS

IN WELSH LANGUAGE

Aros yn gryf, fy anwyl	Stay strong, my darling
Brawd bach	Little brother
Cariad	Dear, Darling
Cariad, dwyt ti ddim	Darling, you are not
Dewch, dilynch fi	Follow me my dears
Ffrind	Friend
Iechyd da	Good health!
Prydferth iawn	Stunning, very beautiful

IN ARABIC (OR TAMACHEQ) LANGUAGE

Allahu Akhbar, salaam alaikum	God is great. Peace be upon you
Ana Assif. Enñe Aátather, sayeedi	I am sorry. I apologise sir.
Assiwi	Herbal treatment, cooked over the fire
Eghale	Beverage made of crushed millet, dates and goats cheese, mixed with water
Guelta	A permanent pool formed when underground water in lowland depressions spills to the surface
Kafir	Infidel, unbeliever
Khanja	Large curved dagger (Omani, Bedouin)
Khanzeer	Pig, swine (derogatory)
Sharaf	Code of Honour (also Bedu)
Tachelt	Snake

IN FULA LANGUAGE

Arawa	Donkey
Baaba	Father (respectful)
Farni	Fried flour dumpling
Nboodi	Snake
Pentat	Guinea Fowl - large African game bird
Yahii	God. The Creator

IN AFRIKAANS LANGUAGE (SOUTH AFRICA)

Aardvark	Badger-sized African burrowing mammal
Ag	Ah
Bliksem	Damn it
Jislaaik	Wow
Koevoet	Controversial and predominantly black South West African Police
Ons het jou kom haal	We have come to fetch you
Troepie	Soldier, private

IN FRENCH LANGUAGE

Auberge	Small hotel/inn
Derriere	Buttocks
Maire	Mayor
Militaire	Military, army

NOTES ON EXPLORERS

The most well known of the early explorers to Tombouctou were:
Alexander Gordon Laing, a Scot who arrived in 1826.
René Caillié, a Frenchman who arrived in 1828.
Heinrich Barth, a German who arrived in 1853.

Published accounts of their journeys can be found in the British
Library and the Deutsche National Bibliothek

 **B B C** NEWS

AFRICA

25 November 2011 Last updated at 20:48

Mali kidnapping: One dead and three seized in Timbuktu

An armed gang of kidnappers has abducted three tourists and killed a fourth in the city of Timbuktu in northern Mali, security sources said.

Two of the hostages are Dutch and the third a South African who may have lived in the UK, reports say. The nationalities have not been confirmed.

The dead man, said to be German, was shot dead trying to resist the gang.

It is believed to be the first time foreigners have been abducted in Timbuktu, once popular with tourists.

However, a group linked to al-Qaeda has attacked Westerners in nearby regions.

Following several kidnappings, **the UK has warned its citizens** not to travel to northern Mali, including Timbuktu.

On Thursday, two French geologists were kidnapped by an armed gang in the eastern village of Hombori.

Police protection
The Timbuktu gunmen burst in as the four were dining in a restaurant on the central square of the ancient city.

http://www.bbc.co.uk/news/world-africa-15895908?print=true   28/11/2011